STINGRAY™

PROJECT ORCA

By Bob Ayres

PART OF THE

STINGRAY™ DEADLY UPRISING SAGA

ANDERSON ENTERTAINMENT

Anderson Entertainment Limited
Third Floor, 86–90 Paul Street, London, EC2A 4NE

Project Orca by Bob Ayres

Hardcover edition published
by Anderson Entertainment in 2024.

Stingray ™ and © ITC Entertainment Group
1964, 2002 and 2024.
Licensed by ITV Studios Limited. All Rights Reserved.

Deadly Uprising ™ and © Anderson Entertainment 2024.

http://www.gerryanderson.com

ISBN: 978-1-914522-78-9

Editorial director: Jamie Anderson
Cover design: Marcus Stamps

Typeset by Rajendra Singh Bisht

Table of Contents

CHAPTER 1	Dead in the Water	7
CHAPTER 2	Rhapsody in Green	15
CHAPTER 3	Pride Before a Fall	25
CHAPTER 4	Attack of the Mechanical Mermen	33
CHAPTER 5	Master of Disguise	45
CHAPTER 6	A Big Brute of a Boat	59
CHAPTER 7	Terror from the Deep	67
CHAPTER 8	The Enemy Within	77
CHAPTER 9	Let the Trials Begin!	89
CHAPTER 10	Stingray for Breakfast?	99
CHAPTER 11	Shakedown	109
CHAPTER 12	The Stowaway	119
CHAPTER 13	The Conquest of Terrainea	137
CHAPTER 14	Weapons of War	147
EPILOGUE	Undersea Friends	159

CHAPTER ONE

Dead in the Water

It was the end for Stingray.

The world's most advanced submarine was dead in the water and she sank slowly to the sea bed, the blue, silver and gold of her once sleek hull dented and scored, bubbles rising from ruptured seams, lights flickering in the windows. Huge shadows loomed around her in the darkness of the ocean depths as unnatural creatures clanked and crawled closer, hungry for the kill.

On board, the bridge shook as Stingray finally hit the ocean floor and settled on the rocks. Smoke drifted throughout the cabin, bright sparks cascaded in bursts from overloaded circuits, water dripped from the roof and pooled along the edge of the tilted deck. Two men wearing the uniform of the World Aquanaut Security Patrol were slumped, barely conscious, over their steering columns.

The younger of the two men, Captain Troy Tempest, groaned and shook his head in an attempt to clear it. He straightened his cap and looked at the older man in the co-pilot's seat beside him.

"Phones? You okay?" he said. Lieutenant Sheridan coughed and opened his eyes.

"I'm here. I'm up. I'm wide awake," he drawled. Troy grinned, and then looked over his shoulder towards the rear of the bridge, but there was too much smoke to see anything.

"Marina? How are you doing back there?" he called. No answer, but then – as Marina was mute – Troy wasn't expecting one. Instead, the wreaths of smoke parted, and a beautiful young woman with long green hair appeared, elegantly and incongruously dressed in long iridescent robes. She limped towards Troy and gripped the back of his chair for support. She smiled bravely and nodded.

"That last blast nearly finished us," said Troy. Phones adjusted his hydrophone headset, joggled the control column in front of him, and pulled various levers with increasing desperation.

"No response," he said, "I think we're done for, Skipper!"

Troy released his safety straps and staggered across the sloping deck to a console on the port side of the bridge. Warning lights were flashing all over it. He pushed buttons and flicked switches, and one by one the lights went out. That wasn't a good sign.

"Everything's fried, and the back-ups aren't cutting in," said Troy and resorted to thumping the console with his fist.

"No propulsion, no missiles, no nothing," confirmed Phones. Then he felt a hand on his shoulder, and turned to see Marina – her eyes wide with terror – pointing out of the front windows.

"Uh... Troy? Any bright ideas? Because now would be a good time," Phones croaked, his mouth suddenly dry.

Troy looked up from the inert console, then joined his two friends to watch a massive red mechanical crab thumping towards them on segmented, pistoned legs, raising smoke-like puffs of sand in the water each time one of the cruel spear-shaped feet stamped down. Two glass domes protruded from the armoured shell, like huge bulbous eyes that glowed amber through the murk, and as the machine approached, Troy could see orange-skinned figures inside, operating the controls. Mounted on top of the monstrosity, as though it was the gun barrel of a tank, a huge fork-shaped weapon was lowering to take aim at Stingray. This was the device that had caused devastation along the Pacific coast, using massive sonic pulses to create artificial tsunamis. And now it was aimed directly at them, about to unleash another powerful blast of sonic vibration. Flanking the tsunami device were several smaller crab machines with gun turrets, and they also scuttled into position to aim their weapons at the stricken submarine. There was no escape.

"Just as well I'm blessed with a happy disposition or the thought of being oscillated to death by a giant crab might dampen my spirits," said Phones.

Troy's eyes narrowed, and he leaned forward to examine the approaching machines more closely.

"That's it! The dampers!" he said, "Marina! Grab that roll of tape and come with me! Phones – standby to blow the ballast tanks!"

"One more blast from that oversized tuning fork and we'll be in itty bitty pieces," said Phones, "and we ain't got nothing to throw at it 'cept stern language!" Then he realised that he was talking to himself.

The giant crab machine was powering up its tsunami cannon. The massive fork began to vibrate, and a deep thrumming noise began. Around the two heavy prongs, circular waves began to form in the water and then shot forwards in an expanding cone towards Stingray. She was helpless before the mechanised monster, like a broken toy abandoned on the sea bed.

Then, on Stingray's prow, the hatch-covers of the forward airlock popped open, and Troy's head and shoulders emerged. He was wearing his scuba gear and holding an empty harpoon gun. He reached behind him and Marina – happily breathing underwater without a mask – passed him a harpoon, on the end of which she'd hastily strapped a grenade.

Troy could feel the deep pulsing of the tsunami cannon in his chest and head, and he was fighting to stay focussed, fighting to stay conscious. He loaded the harpoon, brought the gun up to his shoulder and took careful aim at the giant crab. He pulled the trigger, and the harpoon swished through the water and hit one of the huge shock-absorbing springs on which the fork-shaped weapon was mounted. There was a bright orange bloom as the grenade exploded, and the spring was left dangling uselessly from one end. Troy ducked back down into Stingray's airlock, and the hatch-covers sealed over his head. But the deep thrum of the tsunami cannon continued.

Stingray's bridge was shaking. The drips of water from the ceiling turned to torrents as the submarine was slowly torn apart. Phones pulled off his hydrophones and clutched his head in agony as deep throbs of sound vibrated through his body in sickening waves.

Below deck, Troy and Marina were still in the airlock, waiting impatiently as the water level dropped around them. But then the water stopped draining and they were still waist deep.

"The pumps have failed!" cried Troy, "We'll have to open the door manually!"

They stood either side of the locking wheel and with the last of their strength, managed to turn it and open the hatch. They poured out of the airlock chamber in a gush of sea water, and lay helpless in a large puddle.

"Marina..." gasped Troy, but she was already unconscious. Troy closed his eyes and darkness descended.

But outside, something was happening to the tsunami cannon. The entire length of the tuning fork weapon was beginning to ripple with uncontrollable vibrations. Then the whole crab machine was shaking. It staggered to the left and collided with one of the smaller machines, then lurched to the right, smashing into another. Then the crab reeled backwards, its many mechanical limbs scrabbling and straining to maintain balance. Finally, the legs gave out, and the crab's massive body smashed down onto the sea bed in a cloud of displaced sand. The cannon became dislodged, and – still thrumming with power – collapsed onto one of the glass blister eyes. The orange figure inside threw its hands up in panic as the dome cracked open like an egg. The lights in the machine's eyes flickered on and off, and then...

KA-BOOM!

...a huge magnesium-bright explosion ripped the machine apart and boiled outwards, engulfing the smaller crab machines on either side.

W.A.S.P. headquarters were based at Marineville – a secure site the size of a small town, ten miles inland from the USA's Pacific coast. In the centre of Marineville were three large cuboid buildings, connected by covered bridges and topped by a squat cylindrical Control Tower. Inside, the command staff were waiting anxiously for news.

Commander Shore's hoverchair whirred back and forth, floating an inch off the ground alongside the banks of silent communications consoles. In all his long years of service, Shore hadn't felt so helpless since... well, since his accident. He stopped and spun his chair around to face his daughter.

"Try them again, Atlanta!" he barked.

"Yes, sir," said Lieutenant Shore. She always maintained the courtesy due to her father's rank while in uniform, even if he sometimes forgot that she was also an officer. She switched on her microphone.

"Calling Stingray. Calling Stingray... Come in Stingray. Do you read me? Troy? Phones?... Marina?"

The only reply was the hiss of white noise from the speakers – the same as it had been for the last hour. On the other side of the room, at a wall of tracking equipment, Lieutenant Fisher turned away from a large circular screen and pulled off his headphones.

"Air Support reports a huge underwater explosion near Stingray's last known coordinates!" the young man said. Atlanta's face drained of all colour.

"Oh no!" she gasped.

"But seismometers confirm that the tsunami device has stopped firing," continued Fisher.

"Then they got it!" said Commander Shore. "Get Air Support again! Has any wreckage surfaced?"

Fisher replaced his headphones and turned back to his console, while Shore hovered his chair over to Atlanta.

"Stay strong, honey," he said, "we don't know the full story yet. They might have survived."

"Air Support confirms floating wreckage of undersea machines... and Stingray!" reported Fisher.

"Oh Troy! *Troy!*" cried Atlanta, and burst into tears.

"No... sorry... I mean, Stingray has surfaced along with the wreckage!" said Fisher quickly, "They're okay!"

Suddenly the main speakers crackled into life.

"Tower from Stingray," said Troy's voice, "the tsunami device is destroyed. The immediate threat is over."

Atlanta fumbled with the switches on her desk, and in a voice tight with emotion, she spoke into her microphone.

"Received and understood, Stingray. Are you okay, Troy? And Marina? And Phones?"

"We're all fine, Atlanta," replied Troy's voice, "but Stingray's in bad shape. We used the last of our power to blow the tanks so we could surface before the tsunami device exploded. We're going to need a tow back to base."

"Rescue Launches are on their way, Troy," said Commander Shore, waving at Fisher to organise it, "and congratulations, Captain. Thousands of lives have been saved, and it's thanks to you, to Phones, to Marina... and to Stingray!"

CHAPTER TWO

Rhapsody in Green

The tiny Island of Lemoy lay conveniently close to the stretch of coast about ten miles from Marineville that provided the W.A.S.P.s with their access to the sea. At the top of a jagged cliff, keeping watch over the ocean, stood the island's only building – a large red house that must once have been beautiful and brightly painted but now was neglected and weather-beaten. It looked abandoned. The only movement was at one of the ground floor windows where a peeling white-painted shutter flapped back and forth in the wind.

But floating through the window came the sound of someone playing the piano. And playing it very well. With the accompaniment of a full orchestra.

The drawing room within still retained the faded gentility of a past age. A huge chandelier hung from the high stuccoed ceiling, paintings decorated the walls and long velvet curtains were draped at every window. Around the room, heavy mahogany furniture stood on Persian rugs, and a ponderously ticking grandfather clock was standing sentinel by the door. The far corner was dominated by a grand piano, and a figure sat before it, his fingers dancing over the keys. Surface Agent X-20 was not a pretty sight, even to other undersea people. His silvery-green skin was just a little too sickly, his wide, heavily-bagged eyes just a little too far apart, his blue-green hair just a little too oily. And he looked ridiculous in the traditional long robes of his people. Somehow, he just didn't have the poise to carry them off.

But just for the moment he looked magnificent as he played along to a taped orchestra, lost in the drama of the music. Then the tape ran out and the orchestra stopped. As did the piano, but X-20 continued to mime to the rhapsody in his head, playing a virtuoso performance to the spellbound audience of his imagination. He stood and bowed to their rapturous applause, caught a red rose thrown by an admirer... then the *flip-flip-flip* of the spinning tape reel intruded on his daydreams, and he flopped back down onto the piano stool and stared mournfully at the keyboard. One day he was going to learn how to play this thing for real. With one pale green finger he tried to pick out the tune to Duke Dexter's latest pop smash, but he hit a wrong note, then another, and then lost the tune altogether... and gave up. His shoulders slumped with a deep sigh. Nothing had been going right recently.

He got up and wandered over to the window to gaze out over the wide Pacific Ocean. Part of him longed to go home to the undersea city of Titanica, somewhere out there, far beneath the waves; but he knew he wouldn't be welcome until he fulfilled his job description and provided some useful information that could be used against the land-dwelling terraineans.

His eye was caught by a boat on the horizon, and he idly watched its approach. The thing is, everything he'd done recently had gone wrong, and his lord and master, the Mighty King Titan, Ruler and Saviour of Titanica, was not pleased with him. X-20 could now see there were actually two boats, and they seemed to be heading towards Marineville's coastal installations. What could he do to get back into Titan's good books? One of the boats was towing the other and... X-20 snatched up a pair of binoculars from the window sill.

"Stingray!" he hissed. A W.A.S.P. rescue launch was slowly towing the stricken vessel back to base. So it had survived the tsunami device! How was that possible? As the two craft got closer, X-20 adjusted his binoculars and the familiar dolphin-shaped submarine (why had they called her Stingray?) came sharply into focus. There were large dents in her hull, one of her dorsal fins was missing, and she was listing badly to port. X-20 panned along to the rescue launch, and there on the aft deck, gazing forlornly at Stingray, was that treacherous slave-girl Marina! With her was the ginger-haired clown – what was his name? Phones? – And finally, looking as annoyingly tall, dark and handsome as ever...

"Tempest!" spat X-20. The accursed aquanaut was still alive! But hang on, this was the sort of information that could prove useful.

X-20 dropped his binoculars and stepped over to a particularly ugly painting of two fish on the wall. He pressed a button concealed in the frame, and with a whirr, the picture slid up to reveal an incongruous panel of knobs and switches. X-20 toggled one of the controls and then the whole room transformed: metal shields sliced down to seal the windows; armchairs disappeared behind sections of the wall which flipped around to replace the furniture with computer banks and communications devices; the rest of the paintings slid up in their frames to reveal speakers and flashing lights; and in the centre of the room, a long dining table, complete with candelabra, tipped up and was swallowed by the floor as a large carpeted section turned over on a horizontal axis, and a big control console rolled up to take the table's place. Finally, the whole of one wall, including the sofa that stood against it, slid up into the ceiling to reveal a huge screen. X-20 stood at the central console and took a deep breath. He was just about to open a videophone call to King Titan's throne room, when his hand stopped above the dial. No. This was his excuse to return to the undersea city of Titanica! He would present his valuable information to the Transcendent King Titan in person, and receive his reward!

In the Control Tower at Marineville, Atlanta finished repairing her tear-streaked makeup and snapped her compact mirror shut.

"Er... Commander, would it be..." she began, but her father cut her off.

"I suppose you want to go down and meet Captain Tempest when he comes in?" he said gruffly. Atlanta blushed.

"And Marina, and Phones," she said, "and I want to see what sort of condition Stingray is in."

Commander Shore's face cracked into a rare smile.

"Go on then, Lieutenant," he said, "but I'll want a full report on the status of Stingray and her crew when you get back."

"Yes, sir," said Atlanta, and before Shore could change his mind she walked quickly towards the elevator, giving Lieutenant Fisher a conspiratorial smile as she passed. He grinned back.

"You finished that report yet, Fisher?" barked the Commander. Fisher jumped guiltily.

"Already done and sent off to W.S.P. headquarters, sir," he said, and the videophone beeped.

"Then that's bound to be Washington now," said Shore, and he hovered his chair over to the screen and accepted the call. A grey-haired man with a long, thin nose appeared and frowned out at them.

"Admiral Stern," acknowledged Shore.

"Good morning, Commander," said Stern, in a clipped English accent, "I've read the preliminary report with some concern: it appears that Stingray will be out of action for some time."

Shore gave Fisher a glare before replying.

"We can't be certain of that yet, sir. We'll know more after the engineering team have done a full assessment of the damage and..."

"No, Commander," said Stern, "I want full priority given to Project Orca."

"But Admiral Stern!" spluttered Shore, "After everything Stingray has done for us..."

"Stingray is a tool, Commander," said Stern coldly, "nothing more. And tools eventually wear out and need replacing."

Troy, Phones, Marina and Atlanta stood high up on a metal catwalk looking down into the vast underground chamber of Dry Dock No. 2. Huge conveyors hummed and massive hydraulic arms hissed, and the friends watched as Stingray was slowly lowered with gentle precision onto a waiting steel cradle. The machinery withdrew and a sudden peace descended, broken only by the echoing sound of water and oil dripping from Stingray's battered hull onto the concrete floor. She was a pathetic sight, dwarfed by the cavernous space.

"Oh my," murmured Phones. Marina turned away with tears in her eyes, and Atlanta put a comforting arm around her.

"Don't worry, guys," said Troy, with an optimism he didn't really feel, "Stingray's been through much worse than this!" He paused, trying to think of an example, and then carried on before anyone could contradict him, "and she's the pride of the World Aquanaut Security Patrol fleet! The flagship! They'll throw everything they've got at her, and we'll get her repaired in no time!"

"Yeah, you betcha!" agreed Phones, "I'm sure the damage looks worse than it actually is."

"And we'll all pitch in to help where we can," said Atlanta. Marina smiled, and Troy almost began to believe what he'd said. But then they heard the sound of quick footsteps on the metal catwalk and turned to see Lieutenant Fisher hurrying towards them.

"Captain Tempest!" he called, "I've just heard Admiral Stern talking to the Commander!"

"Catch your breath, Lieutenant!" said Troy, "What gives?"

"The Admiral said that it might not be worth repairing Stingray," gasped Fisher, "this really could be the end of her!"

Agent X-20 had been rehearsing his speech throughout the tediously long journey to the undersea city of Titanica. After his little red and green submarine had settled onto a docking platform, he went through the words one more time while he waited for a travel tube to link up with the airlock.

"Ineffable Titan!" the speech began. Strong start. "At great risk to your humble servant's life, I have managed to obtain intelligence that will be of vital importance in your campaign against the terraineans!" Titan didn't need to know that X-20 had obtained the intelligence by standing at his window. "It is with grave regret..." Regret? No. That made it sound like he could be at fault. "It is with grave *sorrow* that I must report the survival of your Enormity's greatest enemy! The foul Tempest lives!" Too much? No, no, you can never have too much. Now for the really interesting bit: "But during my daring mission... my *death-defying* mission, I also managed to discover that the terrainean weapon of destruction known as Stingray has been damaged – possibly beyond repair!" Excellent. If that didn't get him a seat at the table, then he didn't know what would.

The travel tube took X-20 swiftly into the heart of Titanica where he was met as usual by two Aquaphibian guards. They were nasty, smelly, stupid creatures. Primitive bipeds with deep green skin, protuberant spikes on their heads and down their naked spines, faces like the ugliest of deep-sea fish and brains to match. But they were good at following orders. The guards accompanied X-20 into Titan's audience chamber – an impressive coral pink auditorium that sat beneath a dome of clear crystal, carrying the weight of the Pacific Ocean above them. X-20 didn't like to think about that too much. Huge stone sculptures of fish-gods stood on either side of the throne, where the Mighty Despot himself sat, elevated above his subjects on a circular dais, and backed by a huge pearlescent scallop shell that framed him nicely. X-20 walked confidently into the centre of the room but was annoyed to see that the Great Tyrant already had company. There were ambassadors from several undersea races there, all part of Titan's alliance against the terraineans: cloaked Harmonians with their wide craniums like hammerhead sharks, sharp-fanged Astacus warriors, flat-headed survivors of Starfish City, white-haired Atlanteans... and a few others that X-20 didn't even recognise. It didn't matter – in fact, an audience might help.

"Ineffable Titan!" he began, but his thin, nasal voice was almost lost in the domed chamber, and none of the delegates took any notice of him. Titan gazed down at X-20 with an expression of contempt. He looked at *everyone* with an expression of contempt. He had refined, cruel features, and a short beard that X-20 privately thought made him look like terrainean pictures of the devil. The priestly cap with a pointed widow's peak, and the cape with an elaborately scalloped collar, helped to complete the look, as did the up-lighting on Titan's face.

"What is it, Surface Agent X-20? I do not remember sending for you," said the Imperious Titan in a deep, declamatory, perfectly-enunciated voice. Everyone turned to look at X-20. He tried not to feel belittled by the Glorious Titan's words. He was, at least, the centre of attention now.

"Ineffable Titan!" he started again, "At great risk to your humble servant's life, I have managed to obtain intelligence that..."

"Tempest lives, but Stingray has been put out of action," said Titan.

"...that will be of..." X-20's words dribbled to a halt. Absurdly, he felt like crying.

"How did you know?" he said in a small, child-like voice.

"As soon as contact was lost with the tsunami device," expounded Titan to the whole room, "I consulted Teufel – the Great God of the Sea! And he, in his munificence, informed me of Stingray's fate." Titan gestured magnificently towards a huge glass-fronted tank to one side of the chamber, apparently carved out of solid rock. It was almost completely filled by a very large and very fat fish which was mouthing silently and mournfully at everyone through the thick glass, while its big round eyes swivelled insanely in its head. X-20 groaned inwardly. If you ask a fat fish a yes-no question, and it happens to nod at the right moment, it's going to get the answer correct fifty per cent of the time. In X-20's opinion, it was no way to run a dictatorship, but he kept his expression carefully neutral.

"The loss of the tsunami device is regrettable," continued Titan, "but it has served its purpose! Our alliances with other undersea cities have brought more weapons to my arsenal, and more resources with which to build yet more terrifying machines of destruction!"

This brought a rousing cheer from the assembly. Titan glanced at X-20 and then examined the nails of his right hand as though the state of his manicure was of far more importance.

"Was there anything else?"

All eyes were on X-20 again. He could still save face, demonstrate his worth to these people.

"There is a chance that Stingray will be repaired," said X-20, "or that the terraineans will devise new weapons to replace it! At great personal risk, I shall therefore return to my post, perilously close to Marineville, the lair of the hated aquanauts, and... and..." X-20's mind went blank. "...and find out what's going on," he tailed off.

"Whatever," said Titan with impressive indifference, "But it will soon be immaterial. We have a new plan that will test Marineville's defences, now that they can no longer cower behind Stingray's protection. We will soon see their true mettle in the heat of battle!" Titan's eyes swept the small crowd and fixed on a man at the back of the room.

"Sculpin! Are you ready?" he called. X-20's mouth fell open and he spun around to look. Sculpin?! How had *he* managed to wheedle his way back into Titan's favour? A man stepped forward. He was small, with green-gold skin that deepened to emerald around his dark eyes, making him look like he was wearing a half-mask above his sharply-pointed nose. And at that moment he also looked very smug. In both hands he was holding a red rectangular gadget, the size and shape of a large book, with handles on both sides, a screen on the front, and a circular aerial protruding from the top.

"For some time," said Sculpin in a self-important, whiny voice, "I have been experimenting with electronic implants and signalling devices that enable me to control various sea creatures, and use them as weapons in our fight against the terraineans. Some of you may remember the success I had with the mighty Gargan. Admittedly, the Giant Robot Sea Snails weren't quite as successful as I'd hoped, but that was due to the lack of..."

"I asked if you were ready, not for a lecture," pronounced Titan. A snide chuckle escaped X-20, but he quickly covered his mouth.

"Yes... sorry... very nearly ready, yes," said Sculpin, "The artificers have finished their work, and testing is almost complete. There has been a little trouble with... that is... some of the subjects have... er... *rejected* the process, but we are on schedule to begin Phase One as you commanded."

Titan stood and raised his arms in a gesture that encompassed the whole room, and demanded attention. There was an expectant hush.

"Tomorrow then, Marineville's defences will be tested to their limit! The terraineans dared to claim sovereignty over the seas with their submarines and missiles; but now, with the accursed Stingray defeated, it is our turn! It is time for us, the undersea races, to establish our mastery over the land!"

The chamber echoed with a spontaneous round of applause.

X-20 hurried back to his submarine and was away as soon as the travel tube had disengaged from the airlock. He had to get back to his base on the Island of Lemoy before Sculpin's plans were set in motion.

"Whatever happens, I can turn it to my advantage," X-20 said to himself, "If Sculpin's latest ruse is a success, I can claim it's because I was on the spot to make sure everything ran smoothly. If it all goes wrong – and given Sculpin's track record, I wouldn't be surprised – I can claim it was *despite* my best efforts to help." He chuckled to himself, then stopped. Maybe he should have stayed to find out exactly what Sculpin's plan involved? Never mind. He'd find out soon enough. And so would Marineville.

CHAPTER THREE

Pride Before a Fall

Dry Dock No. 2 echoed with the buzz and clank of heavy machinery and the shouts of engineers as repairs continued on Stingray. Her missing dorsal fin had already been replaced, and now robot arms were lowering a new hull plate into position. A welding machine chuntered forwards on caterpillar tracks, eagerly firing up its bright blue-white torch to seal the edges.

Marina was on board, going from compartment to compartment, clearing away any broken or water-damaged equipment, and making a list of things that would need to be mended. It was already a very long list. She poked her head into the engine room, where two mechanics were having a heated discussion and waving wrenches at each other. It didn't look good. She quickly withdrew, and after dumping another bag of rubbish into the airlock ready for disposal, she climbed up to the bridge. Troy and Phones had removed inspection panels from the various consoles and were both elbows deep in wires and circuit boards. The smell of hot solder hung in the air.

"Hey Marina," said Troy, removing himself from the navigation computer's innards. He had a sooty smudge on one of his cheeks, and Marina resisted the temptation to wipe it off.

"How are you doing with that list?"

Marina handed him her clipboard with what she hoped was an encouraging smile.

"Not as bad as I thought!" said Troy, but then Marina lifted the top sheet of paper to reveal several more pages beneath. She shrugged apologetically.

"Oh," said Troy, "Worse than I feared."

Phones joined them and looked over Troy's shoulder at the list.

"Jeepers!" he exclaimed, "Maybe we should... you know... keep this to ourselves for the time being. If Fisher's right, then the brass hats might decide to cut their losses and send Stingray to the breaker's yard."

Marina frowned and shook her head emphatically. That was NEVER going to happen, not if she had anything to do with it.

"I'm sorry Marina," continued Phones, "but I think Stingray's on borrowed time in any case. Ever since they gave Project Orca the green light. And even if we do get Stingray floating again, who's going to captain her?"

Marina tilted her head quizzically and pointed at Troy.

"It won't be the Skipper," said Phones, "He's the best captain in the W.A.S.P.s! Aquanaut of the Year 2065! Who else are they gonna give Orca's command to?"

Marina turned to look accusingly at Troy, who held up his hands defensively.

"Well look, Marina, I don't know," he said, "I haven't been asked yet, but it makes sense, doesn't it? No other captain in the fleet has my experience: destroying Titan's mechanical fish, fighting Aquaphibians, outsmarting the best brains of the undersea cities."

Marina looked forlornly at the empty captain's chair.

"But I'm still going to need you at my side – both of you," said Troy.

"Gee, thanks, Skipper," said Phones, "but what about Stingray? Aren't you forgetting her?"

Marina nodded in agreement.

"No! Of course not!" said Troy. "We've still got time to get her fixed up! I know it feels overwhelming at the moment, but we've already made good progress. Let's get as much done as we can before anyone notices, and by then Stingray could be seaworthy again. But I agree, let's keep the true extent of the damage between ourselves for the time being."

"Captain Tempest!" barked Commander Shore's voice.

Troy, Phones and Marina all jumped, and spun around to see the door in the aft bulkhead sliding open. From a metal gangplank outside, Commander Shore hovered through the hatch and onto the bridge. He was followed by Atlanta and a tall blond-haired, blue-eyed man with captain's stripes on the epaulettes of his neatly pressed uniform.

"Sir!" chorused Troy and Phones, and they crashed to attention. Shore frowned – they didn't usually stand on ceremony. Never mind.

"Tempest, I'd like to introduce you to Captain Dirk Dune. He's just arrived from Washington HQ and we're giving him the tour. Captain Dune, may I present Captain Troy Tempest, Lieutenant George Sheridan and… er… Marina."

Dune stepped forwards and gave Troy a very firm handshake.

"Captain Tempest," he said in a rich baritone, "Delighted! Atlanta has told me so much about you." He smiled warmly, giving the group a good look at a perfect row of white teeth.

"Captain Dune," acknowledged Troy, noting the new boy's casual use of Atlanta's first name. He wondered precisely when he'd been a subject of their conversation.

Where? And how long for? He gave Atlanta a sidelong glance.

"I was telling Dirk – Captain Dune – how you managed to destroy the tsunami device," gabbled Atlanta, a little defensively.

"Smart thinking, Tempest," said Dune, "spotting the machine's Achilles heel and taking out a damper like that. Inspired!"

"Oh, it was nothing," said Troy modestly, "and it was the Lieutenant's idea, really."

"Indeed?" Dune passed along the row like a visiting dignitary, "Lieutenant Sheridan," he said, bestowing another very firm handshake.

"Call me Phones. Everybody does."

"*Phones?* How amusing," said Dune and moved quickly on to Marina. His smile widened, becoming decidedly wolfish.

"Marina," he breathed, taking one of her hands in both of his, "and what do you do?"

Marina blushed and looked down.

"She can't speak, Captain," explained Troy, and Dune gave a melodramatic gasp.

"The perfect woman!" he exclaimed. Marina was beginning to look uncomfortable, and Troy's voice took on a slight edge as he continued.

"Marina's expert knowledge of the undersea races has been of vital importance to us on our missions."

"A civilian adviser on active service?" said Dune, turning to look at Shore, but not – Troy noticed – relinquishing Marina's hand. "That's most *irregular*."

"It's an irregular situation calling for original thinking," said Shore, bridling at Dune's tone.

"Well, I think it's a wonderful idea," said Dune, his attention returning to Marina, who was gently trying to pull her hand away. "You're a lucky man, Tempest, having such a beautiful companion with you on your voyages."

"Why, thank you kindly, Captain," said Phones, "ain't nobody called me beautiful before."

Dune's blue eyes iced over and he shot Phones a cold, hard stare. But he did – Troy observed – finally release Marina's hand, and she gave Phones a grateful little smile. Commander Shore felt it was time to change the subject.

"Captain Dune has been sent here to oversee the final stages of Project Orca," he said.

"I was personally assigned by Admiral Stern," added Dune, glad for the opportunity to talk about himself. "With Stingray out of action, Marineville's defences have been compromised. Indeed, the safety of the whole world's oceans is at risk, and our new class of submarine – the Orca – is still under construction, so I am here to expedite matters."

"Well, that's very kind of you, Captain Dune," said Troy, "especially as I'm going to have my hands full with Stingray's repairs for the time being."

"Er, Captain Tempest...," began Shore, but Troy was eager to make up for any offence Phones may have caused and kept talking.

"And when Orca is launched, I'm sure your help and advice will be invaluable during the sea trials..."

"My help and advice?" said Dune, raising an eyebrow.

"During the sea trials, yes... having someone there who is already familiar with Orca's systems will be very useful to me."

"Captain Tempest...," Shore tried again, but Dune cut in.

"I think there has been some misunderstanding," he said. "Who do you think will be taking command of Orca?"

"Well, I assumed... what with my experience...," Troy began, but realised that neither Shore nor Atlanta would meet his eye. "Having captained Stingray... the flagship... Aquanaut of the Year..."

Now Phones and Marina were also studying the floor. There was a moment's awkward silence. Then Dune laid a hand on Troy's shoulder.

"Captain Tempest," he said, "I think I speak for everyone in the W.A.S.P.s when I say that you have been a credit to the service. And we thank you. But Admiral Stern feels – and I agree with him – that it's time for some new blood. Shake things up a little. So when Orca is launched, I will be in the captain's chair." Dune gave Troy's shoulder a friendly squeeze and looked around the cabin with a smile as though expecting applause.

"I'm sorry Troy," said Shore quietly, "I only found out myself an hour ago. I was going to tell you..."

"No, that's just fine, sir," Troy said. "Like I say, I've got my hands full with Stingray's repairs anyway."

Dune looked from Troy to Shore and back again.

"Well, I'm sorry to be the bearer of yet more bad news..." he began, but his voice was drowned out by the sound of boots clattering across the metal gangplank and the noisy arrival of an angry-looking lieutenant and two security guards who followed her in through the rear hatch. The cabin was getting uncomfortably crowded.

"Commander Shore!" said the young woman with a conspicuous lack of ceremony, "Who is this man, and why was I not informed of his arrival?" She glared at Dune and stood feet apart with a hand on the butt of her holstered pistol.

Troy, Phones and Marina backed away towards the front of the bridge, partly to make more room, but mainly to get a better view.

"Take it easy, Lieutenant Coral!" said Shore, "This is Captain Dirk Dune – newly arrived from Washington. He has all the necessary clearances."

"With the greatest respect, sir," hissed the Lieutenant, "as Security Officer, his clearances are a matter for me to decide." She held out her hand. "Let's see some I.D, Captain."

Shore looked at Dune.

"May I introduce Lieutenant Sara Coral," he said. "We find it easier just to do as she asks."

Dune, meanwhile, had been examining Sara with undisguised appreciation.

"Charmed," he said, and attempted to take her outstretched hand in his, but she snatched it away.

"I.D," she repeated, but Dune waved her request away as though it were beneath him.

"If you have any concerns, Lieutenant, then may I suggest you take them up with Admiral Stern?" he said evenly. Sara's dark eyes blazed with fury.

"Admiral Stern can..."

But suddenly the sound of a drum tattoo echo-ed around the dry dock from the public address speakers.

"Action stations?!" said Shore and flipped open his wrist radio.

"Shore to Tower! What's going on Lieutenant Fisher? Why have you called Action Stations?"

Everyone listened in as Fisher's voice replied.

"We've got incoming, sir!" His excitement was obvious. "I'm tracking multiple signals out at sea – looks like dozens of small, fast craft all heading in our direction!"

Troy turned and looked helplessly at the tangle of wires spilling out of the various inspection panels.

"Gosh, darn it!" he muttered in frustration.

"Right about now we'd usually be launching Stingray!" said Phones.

"You can still make yourselves useful," said Shore. "Tempest, Phones – you're with me. Captain Dune, I want you to go with Lieutenant Coral, and co-operate with her completely."

"Oh, very well," sighed Dune as though he were doing the commander a favour. He treated Sara to his most charming smile. "It would be my pleasure."

Everyone trooped out of Stingray's rear hatch and onto the gangplank. Only Marina was left on the bridge, listening to the receding hum of the commander's hoverchair and the tramp of boots on the metal grating. She turned to look wistfully out of the cockpit windows, and then sat down in Troy's chair and patted the steering column, offering comfort to her beloved Stingray.

CHAPTER FOUR

Attack of the Mechanical Mermen

In the ocean depths, a fleet of unusual craft slid gracefully through the water, heading straight for the stretch of coastline that lay closest to Marineville. The vessels looked almost like men but were made of brass and steel, and swam without apparent effort, their arms outstretched in front of them in a diving position, powerful turbines in their feet pushing them along at 500 knots. They swooped and twisted around each other as they swam in joyful anticipation of the battle to come.

In Marineville's Control Tower, Commander Shore and Atlanta exited the elevator, followed by Troy and Phones.

"Report!" barked Shore, and Fisher couldn't disguise the look of relief on his face as Atlanta quickly settled at her station on the long central console. Troy and Phones both joined Fisher to look at the circular tracking screen.

"There are twenty submersibles, sir – all about fifteen feet long," said Fisher, "Heading for the coast about a mile south of Stingray's ocean door. If they maintain their present course and speed, they will be at the cliffs in... uh... eleven minutes."

"Stingray would have intercepted them by now," said Troy, feeling like a spare part.

"Any radio contact?" asked Shore.

"None, sir," replied Fisher.

"Very well. Atlanta, keep trying to get through to them, but for the moment we have to assume they are hostile. I am calling Battle Stations!"

"Yes, sir!" said Atlanta and pushed a button on her desk.

All over Marineville, the loudspeakers on every building, signpost and street corner were still broadcasting the Action Stations tattoo. And now another, more insistent beat joined in. People throughout the base stopped what they were doing and listened; vehicles pulled over and awaited instructions. Was this a drill? Then Commander Shore's voice boomed out of the speakers.

"Attention! This is Marineville Control. All personnel stand by for Battle Stations. All civilian personnel to remain in their quarters. All vehicles proceed to nearest ramp area."

Marineville was suddenly a hive of activity. Men and women in uniform double-timed to their posts. Men and women in civilian clothes hurried into their homes. Cars and trucks drove quickly to large parking areas, the borders clearly marked with thick white lines. Everyone knew exactly what to do, and did it exactly as drilled.

In the Tower, Shore watched as one by one, a panel of lights turned green, and then he spoke into his microphone again.

"Five seconds! Five… four… three… two… one… zero!" His voice echoed back at him from outside the building. Atlanta took her cue and spoke into her own microphone.

"Tower to Power-Plant: commence Battle Stations procedure."

PROJECT ORCA

"Battle Stations! P.W.O.R!" replied an engineer's voice.

Marineville held its breath.

Warning lights began to flash and with a deep rumble of immensely powerful machinery, entire buildings began to sink into the ground on huge platforms. The accommodation blocks, the power-plant, the workshop, and the Control Tower itself. The parking areas also lowered underground, each one carrying the trucks and cars downwards like toys on a tray.

Troy and Phones watched as street level rose up past the Control Tower's windows. It wasn't something they often witnessed, and it was awe-inspiring to watch such an incredible feat of engineering in action.

"Emergency lighting!" ordered Shore unnecessarily as the building sank into darkness, and bright white circular lights came on in the ceiling to imitate daylight.

Massive reinforced concrete shutters closed over the yawning gaps where the buildings had stood, and the entire central section of Marineville was now sealed safely underground, re-located in a vast underground bunker.

Ten miles away on the Pacific coast, rolling waves rushed up a narrow sandy beach to crash against the base of the cliffs, churning in white foam before receding, only to gather themselves and crash again and again against the rocks. Then, beyond the breakers, there was a glint of golden light under the water. Something metallic was moving beneath the surface. Then another and another, until there was a long row of submerged brassy objects approaching the beach. The dome of a glass helmet broke the surface, then two more, then all twenty, as the giant machine men heaved themselves upright, and strode through the waves up the steeply shelving beach towards the cliff face. There they stopped and waited until they were all standing in a line facing the rocks. Then, at some unspoken command, they all raised their hands. With a sudden *shink!* long claws extended from their metal gauntlets, and spikes appeared on the caps of their armoured boots. They stepped forward, reached up to dig their clawed hands into the rockface, and pulled themselves up, kicking the points of their boots into the cracks and crevices as they began to climb.

In the Control Tower, Fisher was intently studying his screens and readouts.

"We've lost them, Commander," he announced, "looks like they went straight into the cliffs."

"It doesn't make any sense," said Troy, "What were they?"

"Missiles maybe?" suggested Phones, "But no explosions have been reported."

"And why fire missiles at a cliff face ten miles away?" said Shore. "Anything on the outpost cameras?"

Troy turned to a screen and flicked through the picture feeds from security cameras dotted along Marineville's seaward border.

"Nothing," he said.

"Atlanta, scramble Air Support," ordered Shore, "Let's see what's going on out there."

"No wait, sir!" said Troy, and everyone turned to look at him. He was staring intently at his screen. "I can see movement. There's something coming up over the top of the cliffs. Looks like a person... no... lots of people!"

Phones joined him.

"Switch to Camera 13, Skipper, it'll give you a closer view," he said.

Troy clicked a button and...

"Holy moly!" exclaimed Phones.

"It's an army! An army of giant robots!" said Troy.

Shore, Atlanta and Fisher gathered around them to look at the screen.

"Mechanical fish weren't enough for Titan. Now he's gotten himself some mechanical mermen!" said Phones.

"We can't be sure they've been sent by Titan," rumbled Shore, "But let's not take any chances. Tempest: prepare to launch Interceptor missiles!"

The mechanical mermen were fifteen feet tall, and made of shining brass and steel. They strode smoothly and purposefully across the scrubland in a long line – making away from the cliff top and straight for Marineville. Each merman had a long shiny torso, short, powerful legs and was topped by a bullet-shaped glass helmet that jutted forwards like a beak, its mirrored surface concealing the workings within. But the pipes, pistons and cogs of its moving parts were exposed in all their mechanical glory, and the body-work was engraved and embellished with sea-shell and fish-scale designs. They were like moving sculptures – works of industrial art – and would have been beautiful had it not been for the rack of tubular missile launchers that each merman carried on its back, and the large guns that whirred out of both forearms and clicked into position. They were ready.

"Looks like they're armed and up to no good!" said Phones, still watching the screen.

"Interceptor missile units at green," reported Troy.

All along the coast, in fortified positions under water and on the cliff top, batteries of slim yellow and black missiles swung into position, swivelling and tilting as computers calculated their trajectory.

"Hydromic missiles to launch positions," said Troy.

A safe distance from the centre of Marineville, a large platform rose to ground level. Two red and white launch towers hinged upwards to the vertical position, ready to support the big battleship grey Hydromic missiles that ascended from the silo below.

"Let's fire a shot across their bows," said Shore, "I want a salvo of Interceptors to hit the ground 500 yards in front of them. That should tell us how committed they are!"

"P.W.O.R!" said Troy, and quickly punched the co-ordinates into the targeting computers.

Four Interceptor missiles streaked away from their battery and fanned out, forming a rainbow of exhaust fumes as they curved across the sky, and hit the ground in a perfect line parallel to the advancing row of mechanical mermen. Four loud explosions sent fountains of earth fifty feet into the air, and then shrapnel, stones and soil rained down. The mechanical mermen now knew they were expected, but their only response was to break into a run – smoothly pounding along in a steady rhythm.

"They've increased speed!" announced Fisher, checking his instruments, "They're making 30 miles an hour!"

"Maybe they didn't get the message?" drawled Phones.

"Troy! Another salvo!" bellowed Shore. "This time I want a direct hit!"

"P.W.O.R!" said Troy.

Four more Interceptor missiles roared skywards, reached the peak of a parabolic flight, and started their descent onto the enemy's heads. Four of the mechanical mermen stopped running, and crouched down with one knee and one hand on the ground to give them a stable position. They tilted their bodies slightly, adjusting their aim, and then...

BOOMPF!

Rockets fired from the tubes on their backs and soared straight upwards to meet the descending missiles.

KA-BOOM!

The Interceptors blossomed into balls of dirty orange flame. The four mechanical mermen stood up and resumed their charge towards Marineville, now trailing their comrades by half a mile.

"Again!" bawled Shore, "Two salvos!"

Eight Interceptor missiles screamed down onto the front line of mechanical mermen. Eight of the giants stopped running and knelt down in the firing position.

BOOMPF!

Their rockets launched.

KA-BOOM!

But only six of the missiles were destroyed mid-air. Two Interceptors completed their journey and hit the front line of eight running mermen. Gouts of earth and flame exploded from the ground, and sent five of the mechanical giants flying. They hit the ground with loud clangs and lay still. But three ran on, with twelve more bringing up the rear.

"Sir!" said Troy, "They'll soon be too close to Marineville for us to use any more Interceptors!"

"Then let's stop playing games. Launch Hydromic missiles!" ordered Shore.

This time, all fifteen operational mermen stopped running and assumed the firing position. The huge Hydromic missiles tore down upon them.

BOOMPF!

The rockets launched and met their targets, but the missiles completed their descent and hit the ground with a thunderous explosion.

Even in the bunker, the Control Tower shook and rattled as the shock waves hit.
"Report!" said Shore.
"Looks like they're retreating," replied Fisher.
"What's left of them," added Phones. Troy stood at his shoulder and watched the screen.
"That's strange," he said. "They're taking the damaged ones away with them."
The mechanical mermen that were still in working order had teamed up in pairs to carry or drag their mangled and dented comrades back towards the cliffs.
"You mean they're taking care of their wounded?" said Atlanta.
"They're just machines obeying orders," growled Shore, "Titan doesn't want his technology to fall into our hands."
"Likely use the damaged ones for spare parts too," added Phones.
"Which reminds me," said Troy, "Now the emergency is over, we'd better get back to Stingray."
"I'm sorry I can't give you any more help, Tempest," said Shore. "Admiral Stern has made it clear that getting Orca operational has got to be our number one priority. Without a deterrent at sea, we are vulnerable to more attacks on land."

"You think the mechanical mermen will be back?" asked Atlanta.

"I'm sure of it," said Shore. "This attack was just a test of our defences. Now they know what to expect, they'll try again, and with much greater force."

When Troy and Phones arrived back at Stingray's dry dock, they were met by the team of engineers. They were leaving, and taking their tools with them.

"Hey, hey, hey! Where d'you think you fellas are going?" cried Phones. "Lots of work still to do."

"Ask the new guy," said the chief petty officer, gesturing over his shoulder towards Stingray's bridge. "Says we've been re-assigned to work on Orca."

"You mean Captain Dune?" said Troy, "He can't do that!"

"You take it up with him, sir," said the chief. "We've been given our orders." And he began to walk away with the rest of his team.

"Stay right there, Chief," said Troy, "All of you. I'm going to get this sorted out. Come on, Phones."

And as Troy and Phones stamped across the gangplank to board Stingray, the chief wearily put down his toolbox and sat on it.

"Let's give them five minutes," he said to his disgruntled team.

When Troy and Phones stepped onto the bridge, they were greeted by the extraordinary sight of Captain Dune having a heated argument with Marina. He was doing all the actual arguing, of course, but Marina was more than keeping up her side of the confrontation with fierce facial expressions and wild eloquent gestures.

"Marina, you are not an officer!" Dune was saying, "You have no authority here!"

To which Marina put her hands on her hips and thrust her head forward to stare straight up into Dune's face – she had authority all right. Unfortunately, Dune obviously found the girl's defiance amusing and gave a derisive little chuckle.

"Has anyone ever told you how attractive you are when you're angry?" he said. Marina clenched a fist and shook it in his face, which delighted him even more.

"My, my, you're wild one. Maybe you need taming?" he grinned. Marina drew back her arm and...

"What's going on here?" said Troy. Marina and Dune both turned to look at him.

"I was just trying to explain to your delightful civilian adviser..." began Dune, but he couldn't compete with a furious burst of expressive gestures from Marina, in which she managed to convey her concern for Stingray and her dislike of Dune with admirable clarity. Phones couldn't help laughing.

"Normally I'd be translating 'bout now," he said, "but I think you catch the drift."

Troy wasn't seeing the funny side.

"Captain Dune," he said with forced civility, "I would take it as a personal kindness if you left the members of my crew alone. And I'd also like to know who gave you the authority to re-assign Stingray's engineers to Project Orca?"

"The members of your crew, Captain Tempest?" replied Dune, with a mocking smile, "There are only two of them! I suppose you have to exert your authority where you still can. And the engineers do not belong to Stingray. As the land attack has just proved, we need to stop wasting time with this outdated wreck, and concentrate on getting Orca seaborne. I am only acting in the best interests of us all. And with the complete backing of Admiral Stern, of course."

"You have exceeded your authority, Captain Dune," said Troy, not bothering to conceal his anger, "and I will be taking this matter up with the Admiral myself."

"Do as you wish," replied Dune with a shrug, "but you'll find that he is in complete agreement with me."

"Skipper," said Phones urgently, "they're a-leaving!" and he pointed out of the port windows at the engineers who had picked up their toolboxes and were heading for the exit.

"We've got to stop them!" said Troy, and he hurried off the bridge, with Phones at his heels. Marina hesitated only to aim a furious scowl at Dune, and then ran after them.

Dune was left alone on Stingray's bridge. He gave a deep theatrical sigh and shook his head sadly. Why wouldn't they see things his way? He was right. He was always right. How could he convince Troy, Phones and that *creature* that their stubbornness to accept the inevitable was a waste of time, effort and resources? He looked out of the windows at the three of them desperately pleading with the chief and his gang. What if Troy managed to persuade them to stay? Dune gazed around at the different consoles and instruments in various states of disrepair. I mean, look at it! What a mess. Although he could see they'd managed to finish the rewiring behind those front panels. Dune glanced out of the window to make sure Troy, Phones and Marina were still occupied, then picked up a screwdriver and walked over to remove a forward inspection hatch.

"What have we here?" he murmured to himself.

CHAPTER FIVE

Master of Disguise

On the Island of Lemoy, Surface Agent X-20 stood at the window of his cliff-top house, watching the sea and reflecting on the morning's events.

He had been woken by the bells, klaxons and sirens of various alarms all going off at once, and he'd staggered into the drawing room, still rubbing sleep from his eyes, to find the banks of equipment already rotating out of the walls and floor, with lights blinking, screens blipping and paper readouts chattering reams of data out onto the carpet. He'd silenced the alarms – thank Teufel for that! – and tried to make sense of the readings.

"Twenty submersibles, heading for..." X-20 had abandoned his highly advanced computers, run over to the window and snatched up his trusty binoculars. He'd focussed them on the cliffs that lined the mainland coast and watched with fascination as giant brass robots emerged from the waves and climbed the rock face. Then, a few minutes later, the sky above the cliff top had performed an incredible light show – and the sound of detonations had rumbled across to his island, like thunder following lightning. A final huge explosion had seemed to bring the entertainment to an end, but then a short while later, the brass robots had returned

– some damaged but still operational, some being carried across the shoulders of their comrades as they'd descended the cliffs and returned to the sea.

Now X-20 was thinking about how he could turn what he'd witnessed to his advantage. Clearly, an attack on Marineville had failed, but he was sure that the Indomitable Titan would keep trying – and this provided him with an opportunity. He activated his wall-sized videophone screen and hoped that Titan was in the mood to receive his call. There was an anxious pause, but finally the screen lit up with the imperious face of the Potent Leader.

"Surface Agent X-20!" declaimed Titan, "What have you to report?"

X-20 cleared his throat and began: "The ground attack on Marineville..."

"Has been repelled. I know," said Titan.

"The brass robots suffered..."

"Acceptable losses. I know that too."

"But all of the damaged robots..."

"Were recovered. Yes. Do you have anything to tell me that I *don't* know?" sneered Titan. This wasn't going as well as X-20 had hoped. Again. But he soldiered on.

"Can I assume that this was but the first in a wave of ground attacks on Marineville?" he said.

"You are correct in assuming that," said Titan.

"Then at great personal risk – as ever – I will prove my worth as your best Surface Agent...," X-20 tried to ignore Titan's snort of derision, "...and infiltrate Marineville so that I may help your next ground attack to succeed from the inside."

"And how will you accomplish this feat?" said Titan. X-20 hadn't thought this far ahead.

"Well, you know... I can disguise myself and... spy... and sabotage... er... things," he said. There was a long pause, during which X-20 wondered if Titan had even heard him.

"X-20," pronounced Titan at last, "you are a very long way from being my best Surface Agent. I could name a dozen who have provided better intelligence than you in our recent campaign. But very well. This first attack was a test – both of Marineville's defences and of Sculpin's new technology. Once the 'brass robots', as you call them, have returned and we have analysed the data they bring, Phase Two of my plan can begin. We will keep you apprised, and hopefully – by the time we next speak – you will have thought of something that might actually be of some use to me."

X-20 bowed gratefully to Titan's huge image.

"Thank... oh," he said as the screen went blank. Never mind: to work! X-20 flicked a switch on the central console and on the wall to his left, a bookcase slid aside to reveal a doorway. He walked through into the small room beyond, and looked around with pleasure at the collection of wigs, makeup, costumes and props that he used to disguise himself as a land-dweller. He breathed in deeply to savour the musty smell. He loved this room. He sat down at a dressing table in front of a large mirror surrounded by bare bulbs, and picked up a stick of greasepaint in the disgusting colour of terrainean flesh. He spoke to his reflection.

"Tomorrow I will enter Marineville disguised as one of their own, and help to bring about their final defeat!"

Checkpoint One was now the only way into or out of Marineville – the new Security Officer Lieutenant Coral had seen to that – and so the guards were used to dealing with a steady stream of people and vehicles coming and going throughout the day. Inevitably, they got the occasional crank: protestors, conspiracy theorists, even Troy Tempest fans hoping for a signature. He'd become quite the star since his appearance on the Aquanaut of the Year TV spot.

But for some reason, on the morning after the mechanical mermen attack, they got more than the usual number of eccentric visitors. First there was the window cleaner. The old blue truck drew up to the red and white striped barrier and Sergeant Hank Waterman approached the driver's window.

"Kleen-U-Quick?" said the man behind the wheel.

"Say what?" said Hank. Get a load of this guy, he thought.

"I'm the window cleaner," explained the man. He had wide staring eyes, a pencil moustache and was wearing a blue and yellow uniform cap, perched on top of an extraordinary head of blue-grey hair. Had to be a wig, thought Hank.

"Kleen-U-Quick, you say?" he said, "I think there's been a misunderstanding here, pal. We're using a company called 'Eezee-Squeegee' now, after some mook from your outfit fell off the Control Tower a while back."

"Yes Officer, I'm here to give your windows a complimentary clean – for free, you understand – as recompense for that misfortunate episode," said the man, who suddenly looked very shifty. More shifty.

"No can-do, buddy. All external contractors gotta have clearance from the Head of Security – Lieutenant Coral, and if I let you in without it, she'll have my hide. Try phoning ahead next time. Come on, turn it around."

And so the window cleaner executed a laborious five-point turn, and drove away.

A little while later, a shiny black sedan hovered up to the barrier, driven by a man with wide staring eyes that peered out from behind wire-rimmed glasses. He had a tidy pointed beard and neat cap of red hair with a ruler-straight side-parting. Had to be a wig, thought Hank.

"Clutterbuck," said the man behind the wheel.

"Say what?" said Hank. What were the chances? Two in one morning.

"Mr Henry J. Clutterbuck," replied the man, "I'm from Environmental Health and Safety."

Hank picked up a clipboard from the windowsill of his hut and looked at the list of pre-cleared visitors.

"I don't have your name down here, Mr Clutterbuck," he said. The visitor was wearing a bow tie. A spotted bow tie. Hank was therefore not inclined to be helpful, even if the man hadn't been from Health and Safety. But the visitor was already out of his car and measuring the height of the barrier with a tape-measure.

"No, no, no, no, no," he said, shaking his head. The tape-measure rewound with a snap. "This barrier is an inch and three-eighths too low." He wrote down the figure carefully in a notebook. "A tall person could just step over it! Children might bump their heads!"

Hank didn't think either scenario very likely, and tried to take control of the situation.

"I'm sorry, Mr Clutterbuck, but unless your name is on my list, I can't allow you to enter. Your office should have called to make an appointment."

"But this is a surprise inspection!" said Mr Clutterbuck triumphantly. "It wouldn't be much of a surprise if you knew I was coming, now would it, Officer?"

Hank had to admit he had a point there.

"But everyone has to be given prior clearance by Lieutenant Coral, our Head of Security. If I let you in without it, she'll…"

"…have your hide," completed Mr Clutterbuck, "I know."

"Er… yeah. So you understand how it is."

"And there's no way you'll let me in without alerting Security?" said the man. He looked as though he was about to burst into tears.

"None. Sorry, sir. Now if you don't mind, you're holding up the queue."

And the man sadly got back into his sedan, performed a one-eighty degree turn on the spot, and hovered away.

Finally, there was the Singing Telegram. A bright red scooter trailing multicoloured balloons stopped at the barrier, ridden by a man with wide staring eyes and an untidy mop of unnaturally black hair. Had to be a wig, thought Hank. The visitor kicked down the scooter's stand and leapt off to present himself with a broad, enthusiastic, but slightly desperate, grin.

"Ta-dah!" he sang.

"Say what?" said Hank. Seriously, it was turning into quite the morning.

"Ta-dah!" sang the man again, and spread his arms wide so that Hank could read the words on his bright yellow T-shirt: *Surprise Serenades! Singing Telegrams for Every Occasion!* Hank ignored it.

"What can I do for you, pal?" he said.

"I have a special message for... ah...," the man produced a notebook, "Lieutenant Coral! Sent by her dear friends to surprise her!" and he blew a loud chord on a harmonica.

"Okay. Give me the message and I'll make sure she gets it," said Hank. The man seemed to find this very amusing, and he cackled in a most unattractive way.

"Heh-heh-heh! No Officer, you don't understand! It's a singing telegram! It's a personalised message, set to music, crafted especially for Lieutenant Coral. I have to deliver it in person!" and he played an arpeggio on his harmonica to prove it.

"Sorry, but we're in the middle of an emergency situation here. I can't let you onto the base without security clearance."

"You put me in a difficult position, Officer," said the man mournfully, "I have been paid to deliver a message in person. Lieutenant Coral will be disappointed when she learns that she missed out on a 'Surprise Serenade'. And annoyed at you for upsetting the dear friends who sent it."

Hank considered this. He didn't want to incur Lieutenant Coral's wrath. Not after the last time. The visitor pressed his advantage.

"Just think how pleased she will be with you for using your intelligence and sound judgement to allow her the innocent pleasure of a special message from home."

"Well okay, pal," Hank said, "Give me a moment, and I'll radio Security,"

"Don't do that!" cried the man in alarm, and then quickly recovered his composure. "I mean... Lieutenant Coral is Head of Security, so it might be her who picks up the call. It'll spoil the surprise!"

Hank pushed his white helmet back a little so he could scratch his forehead.

"How did you know that Lieutenant Coral is Head of Security?" he asked.

"Oh...," said the man. "You just said so. Didn't you?"

Hank supposed he must have done.

"Okay, buddy. You got me. Keep ahead on this road, second right, and the Security Office is the first building on the left."

The man from Surprise Serenades looked like he couldn't believe his luck.

"Morning Sergeant. What's the hold-up here?" said Lieutenant Coral, walking up behind Hank.

"Lieutenant!" he yelped, and stamped to attention. He didn't know whether to be worried that Lieutenant Coral had heard him about to let the man into Marineville, or relieved to have his dilemma resolved. Sara Coral gave him a long appraising look.

"At ease, Sergeant, just doing my rounds. Who's this?" she said, turning to inspect the visitor, who had wide staring eyes, a bright yellow T-shirt and an obvious wig.

"It's a message, Lieutenant," said Hank, "A personalised message, set to music, crafted especially for you." He beckoned the Singing Telegram forward. "This is Lieutenant Coral! Ain't that a piece of luck!" He grinned, but the visitor suddenly looked very ill.

"A message?" said Sara, and read the words on the man's T-shirt. "Someone sent me a 'Surprise Serenade'?"

"Ta-dah!" sang the man weakly.

"I was explaining to him," said Hank hurriedly, "that, what with the current emergency…"

"Yes, Sergeant Waterman," Sara cut him off. The general public didn't need to know there was an emergency. She looked back at the visitor who was edging slowly towards his scooter. This didn't smell right.

"Go on then," she ordered.

"Excuse me?" replied the man.

"I said, go on then. Let's hear it."

"Oh… well… right here? Right now?"

"Yes. A personalised message, set to music, crafted especially for me, apparently."

The man looked like a hunted animal. There was no way out of it. He blew a tremulous chord on his harmonica to get the right key and cleared his throat. Then haltingly, to the tune of Happy Birthday, he sang in a thin, nasal voice that made both Lieutenant Coral and Sergeant Waterman wince.

"Lieutenant Coral is swell,
She's so… *moral*… as well,
We want to say how much we love her,
…And we're under her spell."

The man looked both relieved and unaccountably pleased with himself.

"Oh, and..." the Singing Telegram untied the bunch of balloons from the back of his scooter and offered the tangled strings to Lieutenant Coral with a hopeful smile. Sara didn't take them. Instead, she gave the man a sarcastic, slow clap. Unbelievably, he bowed to accept his applause.

"Who inflicted this ordeal upon me?" she said.

"Who did what?" The man was still holding out the balloons.

"Who sent me the 'Surprise Serenade'? The Mauled Melody? The Terrible Tune? I would like to thank them."

"Oh, you know... friends. Close friends from... back home."

"And these 'close friends' call me 'Lieutenant Coral', do they?"

"Well, it's not for me to question the wording my clients choose..."

"And do these 'close friends' have names?"

"I cannot divulge my clients' names if they have requested anonymity." The man looked offended at the very thought. Sara drew her side arm. She kept the pistol pointing at the ground, but the threat was clear.

"Go on, get out of here," she said, "and I never want to see your ugly mug again."

The man from Surprise Serenades hopped onto his scooter, kick-started it, turned and accelerated away in a cloud of blue exhaust and a confusion of balloons. Hank grinned, but then realised that Lieutenant Coral was staring at him. The grin vanished.

"If you ever think of letting someone through these gates without clearance again," said Sara calmly, "you'll be scraping the barnacles off the bottom of every ship and submarine in the W.A.S.P. fleet. Do I make myself clear?"

"Yes, ma'am," said Hank.

About five miles from Marineville, on a straight road that continued on into the desert, stood a restaurant called The Oasis, famed throughout the region for its haute cuisine and excellent service. All X-20 wanted was a drink. He couldn't face going back to his island home, in case Titan called. He slammed through the swinging doors of The Oasis, made straight for the bar and slouched onto a stool.

"What'll it be, friend?" said the barman. What X-20 really wanted was a Titanican Whalehammer, a noxious and notoriously strong spirit distilled from seaweed, but he doubted very much they stocked it here.

"Scotch on the rocks," he said, "Make it a double."

"Yessir, and if you don't mind my saying, you look as though you could use it."

X-20 looked down at what remained of his Singing Telegram disguise. The T-shirt was filthy, and the trousers had a large hole ripped out of the seat.

"I don't want to talk about it," said X-20.

The day had been a disaster. None of his disguises had worked, and he couldn't understand it — they'd been such a success in the past! He was a master of disguise! So after Lieutenant Coral had warned him off in no uncertain terms, he'd considered less subtle ways of getting into Marineville, like climbing a wall, or cutting through a fence, but the place was impregnable. Every wall was topped by spikes, all the fences were electrified, and white-helmeted guards patrolled every yard, some of them with fierce-looking dogs, straining at their leashes. Security had certainly increased recently. Most surprising of all, to the west of Marineville — facing the sea — he'd been stopped in his tracks by a newly-painted sign that read:

PROJECT ORCA

WARNING
DANGER OF DEATH
Mine-fields and motion-activated machine-gun nests beyond this point
DO NOT ENTER

Then, finally, a bit of luck. He'd found a small section of fence where the dirt had been scooped away beneath it, presumably by a wild animal resentful of the barrier across its territory. Careful not to touch the electrified wire, X-20 had wriggled beneath the fence. He'd made it! He was inside Marineville! And he'd scurried into the cover of some bushes. Now all he had to do was...

But suddenly there'd been the sound of whistles, shouting, running feet and barking. X-20 had run back to the fence and just got his shoulders under the wire when a large black dog had sunk its teeth into his bottom. Fortunately for X-20, the dog had clearly not liked the taste of Titanican flesh, and let him go with a whine and a shake of its jowls. By the time the guards had caught up with their hound, X-20 had made his escape.

And now he was in a bar full of terraineans, drinking something that tasted like old rope, and having to listen to lots of spoiled rich people enjoying themselves in the restaurant behind him. X-20 could hear one guy who was making a particular performance of it – speaking in a loud baritone voice and laughing enthusiastically at his own jokes. Curiosity got the better of him, and X-20 swivelled around on his stool to get a look at the source of all the hilarity. A blond, blue-eyed man wearing a shiny tuxedo that showed off his broad shoulders and well-muscled chest was sitting at a candlelit table for two, talking at some poor young woman with reddish brown hair in a short, bouffant style, and wearing a pink evening dress.

"I'm so glad you accepted my invitation to come out tonight," the man was saying, "I think I'd have gone mad if I'd had to spend another evening at the Blue Lagoon. The barman there... what's his name?"

"Luigi," said the woman.

"Luigi, yes, he couldn't mix a decent dry vodka Martini if his life depended on it. And if it were up to me, his life *would* depend on it!"

The woman laughed politely.

"No, the secret is to merely coat the inside of the glass with vermouth," continued the insufferable man, "not drown it in the stuff. And that's why I'm so relieved to have discovered this place and the wonderful Rico." At this he raised his glass to the barman, who smiled and gave a little bow.

The woman turned around with a smile for Rico, and X-20 nearly fell off his stool. That was Lieutenant Atlanta Shore! She worked in the Control Tower at Marineville! She turned back to her companion, and the conversation – the rather one-sided conversation – continued.

"Who's the wise-guy?" whispered X-20 to Rico.

"Captain Dirk Dune," he replied quietly. "He works at Marineville. The W.A.S.P. base up the road?"

"Never heard of it," said X-20.

"I shouldn't really be here," Atlanta was saying, "Sara would be very cross if she knew. Marineville personnel aren't supposed to leave the base at the moment."

"You leave Lieutenant Coral to me!" said Dune, "Rank must have its privileges, after all. And we'll have little time for wining and dining once – you know...," and here his voice dropped infinitesimally, "...once Project Orca is up and running."

"Shh!" said Atlanta.

"Oh, don't worry! Who's going to hear in this out-of-the-way place? But if it makes you happy, we'll call it 'the new vessel' instead, shall we?" And Dune gave Atlanta an exaggerated wink. How many Martinis had he drunk?

"I don't think we should be talking about it at all," said Atlanta.

"The crew will be flying in on Thursday," said Dune, completely oblivious to her concern, "and then it will be all hands to the pump. I'm quite excited, actually. Admiral Stern and I have hand-picked the best people from W.S.P. stations all over the world..."

There was no stopping the man. X-20 just hoped he could remember it all.

CHAPTER SIX

A Big Brute of a Boat

The following day, Troy and Marina were back on board Stingray, doing their best to complete her repairs without the engineering crew. The work was going very slowly, and it didn't help that Phones had gone to get some spare parts from the Quartermaster's store over an hour ago and still hadn't returned.

"What could be keeping him?" said Troy. Marina shrugged, but then cupped an ear with her hand to say – listen! And sure enough, Troy heard boots on the gangplank and Phones appeared, carrying a large cardboard box full of circuit boards, wires, bulbs, valves and transistors.

"Sorry Skipper!" he said, "I had a mighty hard time getting the Quartermaster to part with anything. It's all been ear-marked for Project Orca."

"Did you get what we need?" asked Troy.

"Barely. And do you know what else he said?" Phones was clearly upset. Marina nodded at him to go on.

"He said, 'you can have those parts for now, but if they need them on Orca, they'll be coming to get them from Stingray, and anything else they want.'"

Marina covered her ears in shock. Troy was horrified.

"You mean they're going to cannibalise Stingray for parts?"

"That's what he said."

"Well let's see if we can be as far out to sea as possible before they come for Stingray with their wrenches and screwdrivers. I think we're about ready to give the engine a try."

"You sure?" asked Phones.

"I've been over it a dozen times. We both have. Got to test it some time."

"You're the captain! Let's see what she's got."

Troy and Phones sat down in their chairs and gripped the wheels of their steering columns. Marina went to stand by a bank of dials and indicator lights.

"Switch from the umbilicals to internal power," said Troy.

"Power...," Phones flipped a bank of switches, "...on."

"Engine start."

"Engine... start." A low thrum could be felt, vibrating through the deckplates.

"So far so good," said Troy.

"As the man who fell from the hundredth floor was heard to say on the way down," drawled Phones.

"Acceleration Rate One," said Troy.

"Rate One," confirmed Phones, and the whine of the turbine could now be clearly heard.

"Feels good," said Troy, "How's it looking Marina?" and he glanced over his shoulder to see Marina monitoring the dials. She gave him a cheery thumbs-up. But Phones wasn't convinced.

"Hard to tell, Skipper, she always sounds different in the dry."

"Take her slowly up to Rate Four," said Troy.

"Rate Four," confirmed Phones, and the sound of the turbine rose in pitch.

"Still good!" said Troy, getting a happy nod from Marina. "Okay, Phones, take her up to Rate Six."

"Rate Six," said Phones, and pushed a lever all the way forward. A loud bang made them all duck, and the bridge was suddenly full of black, acrid smoke.

"Power down! Power down!" ordered Troy, and started to cough.

"She's doing that all by herself, Skipper!" replied Phones, and the whine of the turbine quickly descended in pitch and died, to be replaced by the whooshing noise of a fire extinguisher.

"Marina! Are you okay?" shouted Troy, getting out of his seat. The smoke cleared and Marina was revealed, holding the spent extinguisher, her face covered in black smuts from a burned-out display panel, but she seemed otherwise unharmed. She gave Troy a shrug.

"Back to square one," said Phones. "Just as well I got those spares."

The radio crackled, and Commander Shore's voice boomed out of the speaker.

"Tower to Stingray!"

"At least the radio's working," said Troy, and flicked a switch. "This is Stingray, go ahead Commander."

"Troy! I want you, Phones and Marina to get yourselves cleaned up and over to Submarine Pen 1. Captain Dune is going to give you a tour of Orca."

"Well, whoopee," said Phones quietly.

X-20 had returned to his house on the Island of Lemoy and spent the night in feverish activity, getting all the pieces of his new plan into position. It was complicated, and it had been a terrible rush to get everything arranged, but it would work! This time it would really work! He was sure of it. Satisfied that everything was now ready, he put a videophone call through to Titan. Unusually, the tyrant's face appeared on screen almost immediately.

"Surface Agent X-20!" he said, "This had better be important..."

"Oh but it is, it is, your Magnificence," said X-20, "I bring important new intelligence, and have formulated a brilliant plan to take full advantage of the information. It will bring glory to Titanica!"

"I will be the judge of that," said Titan, "But it will have to wait. We are about to launch Phase Two – the second wave of our ground attack!"

"No!" shouted X-20, and immediately quailed at the expression on Titan's face, "That is to say, Wondrous Titan, the success of my plan will depend on precise timing, so I am asking you to delay the next attack by just a few hours."

There was a pregnant pause.

"If you wouldn't mind," added X-20.

"Very well," said Titan, intrigued despite himself. "A few hours can't hurt."

Troy, Phones and Marina arrived at Submarine Pen 1 which – in painful contrast to Stingray's dry dock – was all noise, bustle and purpose.

"Heavens to Betsy," said Phones as they stood on a catwalk and got their first good look at the almost completed Orca. The last time they'd seen her, she was still under construction. An awful lot of work had been done since then, and very quickly.

"Yeah," agreed Troy. Orca was big, about twice the size of Stingray, making her about 160 feet long. So that was why they'd had to use one of these older pens – the ones that had housed the huge submarines of the past. Orca had a similar overall design to Stingray, but with more powerful lines. She was broader in the beam, had much wider fins on either side that looked more like wings, and the turbine was huge. Towards the stern, there were four plexi-glass blisters – two each side – the upper halves of small submersible craft that were docked neatly into sockets in the hull. Two more than Stingray had. A black and white paint job covered most of the hull, but there were some sections of bare metal, all of which gave her a functional appearance despite her sleek design.

Marina shuddered as she took in the sight before her. Orca seemed... *forbidding*, somehow. It was probably all the weaponry. There were four elliptical openings for missile tubes in the bow, rather than two like Stingray, and a cluster of large weapons pods beneath the fins on either side.

"She's a big brute of a boat," said Phones admiringly.

Marina shook her head with an expression of distaste. Orca was giving her a bad feeling.

They walked onto the bridge to find Captain Dirk Dune dressed in an immaculate uniform (did he ever get his hands dirty?) giving orders to a crew of engineers in oily overalls. Marina gave a little shiver and hugged herself – Orca even *smelt* wrong. Metallic. Cold.

"Permission to come aboard?" said Troy. He might as well observe protocol.

"Granted, of course!" boomed Dune magnanimously. "Excellent! Now our intrepid friends from Stingray have joined us, we can get started. Carry on, Chief – there's still a lot to do." And he shooed the engineers away with a casual wave.

"Aye-aye, Captain," said the chief, but unseen by Dune, he gave Phones a wink as he turned to go.

"Commander Shore requested that you three should be given a tour of Orca," said Dune, "And I am more than willing to show her off."

"I bet you are," muttered Phones.

"I should begin by explaining," said Dune, "that Orca's systems are highly advanced and she can be piloted by just one person, but she's primarily a warship, and so for optimum efficiency, she will have a crew of seven – all with defined roles and responsibilities for smooth and quick decision-making in the heat of battle." Dune spread his arms wide. "So, as you can see, the bridge is of a different, more spacious design." He stepped into the centre where there was an impressive black chair on a slightly raised dais, surrounded in front by a small semi-circular console.

"This is where I sit," he grinned, "controlling the show. In front of me, are two seats with steering columns of a sort that you, Captain, and you, Lieutenant, should be familiar with! My Navigation Officer will take one seat, a Hydrophone Operator will take the other."

"So you don't actually pilot Orca yourself?" asked Troy.

"I am in overall command, of course," said Dune, "but I have people to do the grunt work. On my right there's a station for the Weapon System Officer, and on my left a station for the Communications Officer. Below decks there will be an Engineering Officer, and a small galley manned by a cook who will double as the Medical Officer."

"You get a cook?" said Phones with undisguised envy.

"But of course. Orca is designed to be at sea for many months at a time, and it's important that we should eat well."

"Tell us about the Weapons System," said Troy.

"Ah yes," grinned Dune, and rubbed his hands together enthusiastically, "Orca has a complement of forty Killer missiles, far more powerful than your little Sting missiles, and with state-of-the-art guidance technology. All we have to do is program a target, fire the missile, and it will find its mark every time. We also have a sonic cannon, two ray guns, and a Camouflage System that will render Orca virtually invisible to sonar and even to the naked eye."

"Please state course heading and speed," said a polite female voice out of nowhere. Dune spun around to see Marina standing beside the Navigator's seat, stabbing at buttons, trying to turn the voice off.

"Please state course heading and speed," repeated the voice. Dune stepped across and hit the correct button to silence it.

"And the delightful Marina has discovered Orca's talking automatic bosun."

"You mean she talks back?" said Phones, "Gee. I'm not sure if I could handle that."

Marina glowered at him and stomped pointedly away to the rear of the bridge.

"Fortunately, you will not be called upon to find out," said Dune. Phones opened his mouth to reply, but Troy stepped in diplomatically.

"I noticed outside that Orca also has four Aquasprite submersibles, rather than just the two we have on Stingray," he said.

"Indeed, although they are called Aquapods – they're larger than your little one-man Aquasprites. Each one holds two people in case the crew needs to evacuate Orca. Although of course, I don't envisage that ever happening."

"It's all very impressive," said Troy.

"Isn't it?" agreed Dune. But Phones was examining the various control panels with a frown.

"I don't see a science station," he said, "Where's the survey equipment and the experimental instruments that Stingray uses for exploration?"

"Oh, they were on the original plans, but I didn't see the need," Dune waved a hand dismissively. "The priority was to get Orca battle ready."

"What's bothering Marina?" said Troy. They looked aft, where Marina was circling the area that – on Stingray – had comfortable seating, a coffee table and bookshelves. Here on Orca, there were racks of automatic rifles and pistols. Marina looked at Dune and folded her arms. She didn't like it. Dune actually rolled his eyes.

"And there's no lounge either," he said, "Orca is a weapon of war. Not a vessel for joyrides and undersea tea-parties. Shall we continue the tour? Lots to show you."

"Now just you wait a minute...," began Troy. But he was cut off by the drum tattoo of the Action Stations signal echoing around Submarine Pen 1.

"Not again!" said Phones. Dune tried to hide his relief, and flipped open his wrist radio.

"Dune to Tower. What's going on?"

"Shore here," growled the commander's voice, "Looks like another attack. Only this time we've got *fifty* mechanical mermen heading our way! I am calling Battle Stations! Anything could happen in the next half hour!"

CHAPTER SEVEN

Terror from the Deep

Deep beneath the waves of the Pacific Ocean, in a dark chamber hidden somewhere within the city of Titanica, Sculpin was trying hard to concentrate on the controls of his new mechanised soldiers. The circular aerial on top of the red book-shaped device was revolving slowly as he relayed commands using toggle switches and buttons on the sidehandles. But he couldn't help but feel distracted, what with King Titan, the Empyreal Despot himself, literally looking over his shoulder at the small screen on the front of his device.

"And this enables us to see what they are seeing?" said Titan.

"Indeed, your Majesty," replied Sculpin, "Each unit has a videophone camera built into the breastplate."

The screen showed a brass and steel man-shaped machine flying through deep water, arms outstretched in front, a white spume churning from its feet as the turbines in its legs powered it along at extraordinary speed. But the mechanical marvel didn't swim in a straight line – it weaved and spun on its axis, almost as though it were enjoying itself. The view changed as the machine whose camerafeed they were watching corkscrewed through the water, bringing more of the metal giants into view, swimming above and below it.

"Fascinating," said Titan, "What awesome creations they are! You have done well, Sculpin! I thought I might have to dispense with your services after those disastrous Giant Robot Sea Snails of yours. Terrible idea. But you have redeemed yourself with these beautiful inventions. That fool X-20 called them 'brass robots', but they are so much more than that!"

"Why thank you, your Highness," said Sculpin, "Mere robots would not have the intelligence needed to be efficient soldiers."

"They retain a measure of independence?"

"A very small amount. My device cancels freedom of thought, and overrides the ability to make any decisions that are not part of my pre-programmed assault plan, but they can improvise within that. The fight or flight instinct cannot be entirely controlled but that can actually be used to our advantage."

On the screen, Titan and Sculpin watched water dripping down the camera lens as the machine emerged from the waves and walked up the beach towards the cliffs.

"The timing is perfect," said Titan, "the attack should begin precisely when X-20 requested that it should. I hope the delay was worth it."

Back on Orca's bridge, Captain Dune dramatically slapped a fist into the palm of his other hand, making Marina jump.

"Damnation!" he exclaimed, "We're standing in the most sophisticated piece of weaponry ever devised, and yet we're helpless!"

"Now you know how we feel," said Troy, "We'd better get up to the Tower and give the commander a hand."

"He's already called Battle Stations," replied Phones. "Everything over yonder will be below ground by now. Let's take the tunnels."

"I'm afraid I can't allow that," said Dune, and stepped over to the Comms console to press a button.

"What do you mean, you can't allow it?" said Troy as a klaxon echoed around Submarine Pen 1. Phones went quickly to the windows to see huge bulkhead doors rumbling across the exits, and sealing with resounding thuds.

"He's activated the Emergency Lockdown procedure!"

"Why'd you go and do a thing like that?" said Troy.

"I think it's our duty to remain here," blustered Dune, "ready to defend Orca, should the enemy manage to breach Marineville's defences!"

"And meanwhile, you don't have to get your hands dirty with any actual fighting," muttered Phones.

"Well, let's hope Atlanta and Fisher can cope on their own," said Troy, "because now we're stuck in here until the emergency is over."

"Sir! Fifty mechanical mermen have reached the top of the cliffs and have begun their advance," reported Lieutenant Fisher.

"Interceptor missile units at green, Hydromic missiles to launch positions," reported Atlanta.

Commander Shore hovered along the Control Tower's instrument banks to study the various screens.

"Fire Interceptors!" he barked.

"P.W.O.R!" said Fisher.

Titan and Sculpin watched the screen on the control device. The image was bumping up and down as the mechanical giant that housed the camera ran towards Marineville.

"They've launched defensive missiles!" said Titan, as the screen revealed white vapour trails pouring across the sky.

"Do not worry, Sire," Sculpin soothed him, "The rocket launchers on the suits' backs will take care of the missiles. I have improved their accuracy, power and penetration."

As he spoke, the screen flashed white as the descending Interceptors exploded harmlessly in mid-air, well above their intended targets. Sculpin checked his readings.

"All fifty suits still operational," he reported.

"Sir! We have inbound air-traffic requesting instructions," said Atlanta.

"I clean forgot! Orca's crew is flying in today," rumbled Shore, "There'll be planes and helicopters arriving from W.S.P. stations all over the world! It isn't safe for them to land here. Divert them all to the airbase at Arago Point."

"Yes, sir!" said Atlanta.

"Mechanical mermen still advancing! No enemy casualties!" reported Fisher.

"Give them all we've got! Fire all Interceptor batteries!" ordered Shore.

"P.W.O.R!" said Fisher.

"I've had enough of this," grumbled Troy, and he walked to the gun racks at the rear of Orca's bridge. "We can get up to the surface using one of the old fire-escape staircases. It'll be sealed at the top, but I'm pretty sure we can get out by one of the air-ducts. Once we get above ground, it's a hundred-yard sprint to the south bunker doors, and then we can get to the Tower and do something useful." He picked up a rifle and checked the magazine.

"Do you mind?" said Dune, "That's one of my guns. It's brand new."

Phones also picked up a rifle.

"Come on Marina," he said, "you'd better stick with us."

As the Stingray crew headed out of the aft hatch, Dune watched them go. Infuriating people. They'd be down at the Blue Lagoon tonight, bragging about their heroic dash to the Tower. No doubt they'd save the day. As they always did. He sighed and reluctantly picked up a rifle.

"Wait for me!" he called.

"Mechanical mermen still advancing! No enemy casualties!" reported Fisher.

"Launch Hydromic missiles!" said Shore.

"P.W.O.R!"

Sculpin's screen went blank.

"What happened?" demanded Titan.

"Hydromic missiles!" said Sculpin, "Eight... no *nine* of the armoured suits are out of action."

He switched to the camera-feed of a different machine, and the screen flickered back on. Marineville was so close now.

"Only nine enemy casualties!" reported Fisher, "Forty-one mechanical mermen still advancing!"

"They're too close to Marineville!" said Shore, "We daren't use any more missiles. Activate automated ground defences!"

"P.W.O.R!"

Troy kicked out the grille of a huge air duct and emerged above ground, followed by Phones and Marina, breathless from climbing up the deep stairwell, and covered in dust from the air shaft. In the distance they heard the crackle of gunfire. Marina looked at Troy, her face white with fear.

"Don't worry, Marina," he said, "That'll be the motion activated machine-gun nests. Must mean that the mechanical mermen have got in under our missiles." There was a loud *crump!* of an explosion, then another and another.

"And that'll be the minefield," added Phones.

"Come on," said Troy, "we'd better get to those bunker doors." And they broke into a run.

"Wait for me!" shouted Dune, bursting out of the air duct behind them.

"Eleven more mechanical mermen down, thirty still advancing!" said Fisher, his voice high with tension.

"What happens if any of them get through the minefield?" asked Atlanta. There was no answer from Shore for a moment, and then he lifted his microphone and pressed a switch on his chair to speak through the public address system.

"Attention! This is Marineville Control. We are under attack by ground forces approaching from the west. All security guards to defensive positions, draw arms and prepare to engage. All W.A.S.P. personnel below ground with weapons training report to the armoury where you will be assigned small arms and deployed to security stations on the surface. All civilian personnel remain in your quarters."

Shore switched off his microphone, and sagged back in his hoverchair, apparently exhausted. Atlanta glanced over at her father with concern. She had never seen him look so worried... so *old*.

"Sir!" said Fisher, "Requesting permission to join the fight above ground!"

"Request denied, Lieutenant," replied Shore. He straightened up in his chair. "I need you here. But thank you. And I'm sure Lieutenant Coral is more than capable of looking after herself."

Fisher blushed bright pink, and turned his attention back to the screens without another word.

Titan was laughing as he watched the carnage on Sculpin's screen. They'd lost the signal from several more of the suit-mounted cameras as motion activated machine-gun fire had ripped through the invasion force. Yet more cameras winked off when the suits had entered the minefield, and the ground had erupted all around them. Sculpin found his lord and master's glee unsettling, even though it looked like twelve of the units had now made it through to Marineville's perimeter fence.

"Victory is within our grasp!" proclaimed Titan, as – on screen – two clawed hands reached out for the fence. Blue arcs of electricity flickered and spat as thousands of volts passed harmlessly through the insulated armour, and the chain-linked wire was torn apart like paper.

"Get down!" yelled Lieutenant Coral, as Troy, Phones and Marina sprinted towards her position in front of the south bunker doors. Two mechanical mermen appeared around the corner of an outbuilding. They were huge! Even bigger than expected. Towering giants of glinting metal with cogs and pistons spinning and pumping in their limbs as they approached with surprising grace and speed. Guns whirred and clicked into position on their forearms, and they opened fire.

BUDDA-BUDDA-BUDDA!

Bullets thudded around Stingray's crew as they dived for cover behind a low wall, still twenty yards short of the bunker doors. Sara and two white-helmeted guards returned fire and sparks flew as the shots ricocheted off the mermen's brass armour.

As the mechanical giants turned away from Troy, Phones and Marina to aim a barrage at Sara and her men, Captain Dune hurled himself down behind the wall.

"I said wait for me!" he panted, but no one replied. Troy and Phones raised their heads above the wall, shouldered their rifles and joined the firefight. But...

SPANG-SPANG-SPANG!

...the bullets seemed to have no effect. One of the mermen spun back around to face Troy and Phones, and they just had time to duck before the top of the wall exploded in a shower of brick-dust.

"We're going to die!" whimpered Dune. Marina gave him a frown. He wasn't helping.

"Fire in the hole!" shouted Sara and lobbed a grenade at the other merman.

"Stay down!" hissed Troy, and put a protective arm around Marina's shoulders. There was an ear-splitting bang and the giant machine staggered backwards a few thudding steps, cogs spinning, motors whining and pistons hissing as it tried to regain its balance. Finally, with arms whirling, it fell with a loud clang onto its back. The other merman halted its advance on Troy's position and turned towards its fallen comrade. Troy and Phones popped back up from behind the wall and opened fire, but the merman seemed completely oblivious to the shots as it bent down to help its brother-in-arms.

"Aim for the helmet!" shouted Troy, and shot several rounds at the mirrored dome that was now angled towards him. It shattered, and large shards of glass smashed onto the ground at the merman's feet.

The machine straightened up and looked straight at Troy. A grinning face with dark eyes was revealed beneath the broken helmet. There was a living creature inside the armour! Troy and Phones both stopped firing and stared in horror, their minds trying to process what they were seeing. Above the tooth-filled beak, a metal plate was grafted onto the side of the beast's smooth-skinned, hairless head. Wires and tubes trailed from plugs and sockets in the plate and disappeared inside the neck of the armour. The creature made an odd chittering, clicking noise that made Troy's skin crawl. But Marina was staring at it with tears running down her cheeks. The poor thing was terrified.

"It's a dolphin!" said Phones, "An armoured dolphin!"

"It'll be canned fish when I've finished with it!" said Dune. Now the shooting had stopped, he'd finally raised his head above the wall. He aimed his rifle at the dolphin's exposed head and squeezed the trigger. Marina threw herself at him and – bang! – the shot went wide.

"Get out of my way, you witch!" snarled Dune, and tried to take aim again, but Marina was wrestling with him for the gun. The armoured dolphin seemed to come to its senses. With a disturbing snickering sound, it returned to its friend and pulled it up onto its robotic feet. Then they both turned and ran, pounding smoothly and with astonishing acceleration, back between the outbuildings and away from Marineville.

Sculpin helplessly watched his screen as he flicked through each camera feed. All of the surviving armoured dolphins were breaking off the attack, and helping their fallen pod members back towards the sea.

"I'm sorry, Benevolent Titan," he said, "but the instinct for self-preservation is too strong. I won't be able to reassert control until adrenaline levels have returned to normal, but by then, they'll be nearly back in Titanica."

"No matter, Sculpin. You have done well!" said Titan, "I will long cherish the look on the accursed Tempest's face when he finally realised the true nature of our mechanical soldiers!"

"And I suppose we must thank the slave-girl for saving that suit for us!" said Sculpin, "We can always process more dolphins – we've got plenty of them in captivity – but the armour takes time and valuable resources to build."

"Indeed Sculpin," agreed Titan, "and I calculate that we will need many more suits for our next attack, and the final phase of my plan."

"They are under construction as we speak, Victorious Titan! And next time, Marineville will fall before their might!"

CHAPTER EIGHT

The Enemy Within

Commander Shore sat at the head of a long chart table in the Plotting Room which was in the Tower, next door to the Control Room. In attendance around the table were Captain Troy Tempest, Lieutenant Phones Sheridan, Marina, Captain Dirk Dune, and Lieutenants Atlanta Shore, Sara Coral and John Fisher.

"And thanks to Tempest," the Commander was saying, "we now know that the mechanical mermen are in fact dolphins in armoured suits that give them arms and legs to move around on land."

"But why would dolphins attack us?" said Atlanta, "They're usually so friendly."

Marina nodded enthusiastically and tapped the side of her head.

"Yeah, Marina's right," said Troy, "the one we saw had some kind of implant, surgically attached to its skull."

"You think the dolphins are being controlled in some way?" asked Shore.

"Yeah, it was terrified," said Phones. "Like it was calling for help."

"Nonsense!" scoffed Dune, who had decided it was time he took control of the meeting. "The surgical implant is clearly the way the dolphin controls its suit, and it was terrified because I had it in my sights. I would have killed it too, had it not been for the actions of this... undersea *civilian.*"

Marina glowered at him. Dune paid her no attention and continued.

"Now we know that the helmet is a weak point, I recommend that all security personnel be issued with bazookas. If there's another attack, that should take care of the situation."

Marina shook her head angrily.

"You want to give anti-tank rockets to untrained security guards?" said Sara.

"Well, train them then. You're Head of Security – see to it," snapped Dune.

Sara frowned, took a deep breath and was about to reply, when Shore intervened.

"Thank you, Captain Dune – we'll look into that," he said, but Marina was shaking her head again. She pointed at Atlanta, to the PA speaker on the wall and then she covered her ears and pulled a pained expression.

"What's that, Marina?" said Phones, "You got a better idea?"

Marina smiled and nodded, and went through her mime again: she pointed at Atlanta, to the PA speaker, covered her ears and pulled a face.

"Something to do with me?" said Atlanta, "I'm sorry, I don't understand."

Dune gave a derisive snort. "The girl's mad. She deliberately prevented me from shooting the armoured dolphin. She even attempted to take my gun off me. Clear case of insubordination."

"As you're fond of reminding us, Captain," said Troy, "Marina's a civilian, so she can't be insubordinate."

"Well quite," continued Dune, "I mean, what's she even doing here? How do we know we can trust her? She is, after all, from one of the undersea races. They aren't like us. She'll have divided loyalties – as she's proved quite clearly today. It is my recommendation that she should be confined to quarters until this emergency is over."

The room was suddenly hot with anger.

"Why you lowdown, good for nothing, yellow-bellied, big-headed sneak!" shouted Troy.

"You better hush your mouth right now, Dune, or I'll show you insubordination," bawled Phones.

"Oh Dirk! To think I went to the Oasis with you!" cried Atlanta.

"You went on a date with him?!" wailed Troy.

"You broke the security curfew?!" yelled Sara.

"BE QUIET!" roared Commander Shore.

"Sir," said Fisher.

"QUIET!" barked Shore again. In the sudden seething silence, they all became aware of the videophone beeping.

"There's a call from Washington, sir," said Fisher meekly. Shore glared at him, and then pressed a button on his hoverchair. The wallscreen lit up with Admiral Stern's long-nosed face, and he started speaking without ceremony.

"Commander Shore, I've just been reading your account of this morning's events and I am relieved to note that there were no casualties amongst Marineville's personnel."

"Yes, sir. Thank you, sir," replied Shore. "We've been discussing…," but Stern continued over him.

"However, I have also received a disturbing report from Captain Dune."

Everyone in the room glowered at Dune, who smiled and addressed the screen.

"Thank you, Admiral Stern, and I have just made the recommendation that Marina of Pacifica should be confined to quarters."

"With respect, sir...," tried Shore.

"I think that is a sensible precaution in the circumstances," said Stern. "Captain Dune's report describes how he heroically cornered and defeated two of these armoured dolphins..."

"He what now?" said Phones.

"...and had it not been for the interference of this undersea interloper, this *Marina*, then Captain Dune would have been able to kill or capture the creatures for further study."

Marina shrank inside herself, and stared fixedly at the table.

"Sir, I must respectfully object!" said Troy, "I can personally vouch for Marina's loyalty."

"Goes for me too," said Phones. "Sir," he added as an afterthought.

"If I may?" said Dune, and continued without waiting for permission, "I think Admiral Stern has made a wise and fair decision regarding Marina."

Shore glared at Dune, barely controlling his anger. The captain continued.

"But we must move on to more important issues. It is imperative that Orca is launched without further delay. This morning's attack has highlighted how vulnerable we are without adequate sea defences."

"Indeed," said Stern, "What is the status of Project Orca, Commander?"

Shore took a deep breath in an effort to calm himself.

"Subject to final checks, Orca is scheduled for launch tomorrow," he said. Troy and Phones exchanged a glance. So soon?

"Orca's crew had a brief layover at Arago Point during the armoured dolphin attack," continued Shore, "but they'll be flying over to Marineville later this afternoon."

"Excellent!" said Dune, and rubbed his hands together, "I think a little reception party is in order, don't you?"

Everyone looked at him in silent disbelief.

The door to the apartment burst open and Marina stamped across the living room to the window. She stared out of it with her arms crossed, keeping her back to the door as Sara followed her in, a white-helmeted security guard at her heels. Sara turned and waved the guard back out of the apartment.

"No, no, no – I don't want you in here," she said to him, "Stay outside."

The guard left obediently, and Sara walked up behind Marina and laid a comforting hand on her shoulder.

"Marina, I..."

But Marina shook her off and began pacing up and down the room like a caged lioness.

"I'm so sorry," said Sara, "I feel awful about this."

Marina halted, threw Sara a sarcastic eye-roll, then resumed pacing.

"Yes, point taken, not as awful as you must be feeling, obviously," said Sara. Marina ignored her and continued to wear out the carpet.

"None of us believe you're... whatever it is that Captain Dune is accusing you of," tried Sara, "but he's got Admiral Stern wrapped around his little finger, and orders is orders. Look – if there's anything you want – food, books, videofilms, just tell... just write it down on a piece of paper and give it to the guard on the door. I'll see you get it. And I'll also do my best to get you out of here and back to Stingray."

Marina suddenly stopped pacing and grabbed Sara in a tight hug, burying her face in the Lieutenant's shoulder.

"Ooof! You're stronger than you look! Anyone ever tell you that?"

Lieutenant Fisher stood at the edge of the room with a drink in his hand and looked around at the milling crowd that filled Commander Shore's apartment. No one (apart from Captain Dune) felt like partying, but Shore had insisted that his entire team should attend the drinks reception for Orca's new crew. Apart from Marina, of course. Secretly, Fisher felt very excited to have been invited, to be considered part of the commander's inner circle, and he'd enjoyed getting dressed up in his tuxedo for the occasion.

But the party was not going well. There were two distinct groups: at one end of the room, Captain Dune was holding court to his new crew, who were gathered around him and laughing at all his jokes; at the other end, everyone else stood (or sat) gazing morosely into their drinks – Commander Shore, Troy, Phones and Sara. Sara looked amazing in her long sky-blue evening gown, despite the scowls she kept aiming at Dune and his crew. Atlanta stood in the corner by the record player, having chosen to be in charge of the music rather than have to talk to anyone. Especially not to Captain Dune. Fisher edged towards Sara, and felt a thrill when she turned towards him with a welcoming smile.

"Hey John," she said.

"Hey Sara," replied Fisher, "You look beautiful this evening."

"Only this evening?" said Sara, tilting her head.

"Well, gee... I mean... you always look beautiful. Obviously. It's just not appropriate to say so when you're in uniform."

"And it's appropriate now?" said Sara, frowning.

"Oh. Sorry. I didn't mean to..." began Fisher. But Sara grinned and slapped him playfully on the shoulder.

"Lighten up, John. Just messing. And you look beautiful too."

Fisher blushed.

"Well, at least you're looking a little happier now," he said, but Sara's smile immediately vanished.

"I am *not* happy," she snapped.

"Ah, no. Marina. Can't have been easy to confine her to quarters."

"No, it wasn't. Captain Dune is happy enough for me to do his dirty work when it suits him, but here we are, sharing drinks and nibbles with a bunch of strangers who haven't been through my security procedures because Admiral Stern's blue-eyed boy over there felt it was more important to have a party."

"Oh." Fisher didn't know what to say. Suddenly, there was an insistent ringing sound and everyone turned to see Captain Dune, standing in the middle of the room, tapping the side of his empty Martini glass.

"Ladies and Gentlemen!" he said, "If I could have a moment of your time! Firstly, I must thank you for being here at the end of what has been a very difficult day for us all."

"More difficult for some," muttered Phones. Dune pretended not to hear him.

"But I'm glad you could be here to welcome our new friends – Orca's wonderful and very talented crew!" Dune applauded himself, and the new personnel joined in enthusiastically. At the other end of the room, only Commander Shore attempted to clap, but by the time he'd put down his glass, it was too late. He picked up his glass again. Captain Dune continued.

"Orca's crew are the best of the best..." he said, and Troy coughed noisily.

"...hand-picked by Admiral Stern from W.S.P. stations across the globe," continued Dune. "This is the first time we've actually met in person, so I wonder – would you mind introducing yourselves? I'll get the ball rolling: Hello! I am Captain Dirk Dune, in overall command of Project Orca." He looked around the room, bestowing a smile on everyone, then turned to the man standing beside him, "Choppy, if you would?"

"Yes indeed! Delighted!" said the man with an upper-class English accent. He had short, wavy brown hair with a side-parting, a neat moustache and thick horn-rimmed glasses that made his eyes look unnaturally large.

"I am Loo-tenant – as you chaps insist we say! – Loo-tenant Commander Christopher Waters from England. Friends call me 'Choppy'. Choppy Waters, what? Ha!"

Fisher couldn't help noticing the look of frank amazement that passed between Troy and Phones. The man continued.

"I will be the Navigation Officer and Captain Dune's XO – that's 'Executive Officer'," he helpfully explained with glances towards Sara and Atlanta.

Next, a tall middle-aged woman with a blonde ponytail stepped forward.

"G'day. I'm Lieutenant Commander Sandy Beach from Australia – I'm the Engineering Officer."

Then it was the turn of a tall, thin Black man.

"Hello, I am Lieutenant Bilal Bahari from Kenya," he said, "and I will be Orca's Hydrophone Operator and Helmsman. Pleased to meet you all."

A young South Asian woman with her hair in a long thick plait gave everyone a wave.

"Good evening. My name is Lieutenant Jaladhi Talwar from India," she said, "and I am Orca's 'Wizzo' – the Weapons System Officer."

After her, an Asian man with short grey hair.

"I'm Lieutenant Shui Hai from China – Communications Officer."

And finally came a man with thick, dark hair and an impressively large moustache with waxed tips that curled up over both cheeks. Sara's eyes narrowed.

"Et enfin! Je suis... pardon!... I am Chief Petty Officer Henri La Plage," said the man with an outrageously thick French accent, "and I am zer Medical Officer and – très importante! – le chef! Zer cook!"

"And if you hadn't already guessed, he's from France!" said Captain Dune, and the crew all laughed uproariously.

"You have got to be kidding me," muttered Sara. "That's the most obvious disguise I've ever seen!"

It took all of Fisher's powers of persuasion to stop Sara arresting Henri La Plage on suspicion of being a spy right there and then. Nevertheless, she insisted on leaving the party immediately to complete what security checks she could, using the massive computer in her office. Fisher was delighted that Sara seemed to take it for granted that he would accompany her. She punched her information request into the computer keyboard with unnecessary force, and they waited in the darkened office while the machine hummed and chuntered, gathering data from W.S.P. computers all over the world.

"I should have seen the new crew's security files before they even set foot in Marineville," said Sara.

"Do you read everyone's security files?" asked Fisher, "Even the personnel who were already here when you arrived?"

"Everyone's. And that reminds me: you've been keeping a dark secret, haven't you?" Sara frowned at Fisher. His mind raced.

"You thought I wouldn't find out, didn't you?" she said. What could she be referring to?

"Your middle name is 'Horatio'!" Sara grinned, and Fisher laughed with relief.

"You clearly have a guilty conscience," said Sara. "It was fun to see you squirm."

"I suppose, with 'Horatio' for a middle name," mused Fisher, "it was inevitable that I'd end up in the World Navy or the W.A.S.P.s. One of the two."

"I'm glad it was the W.A.S.P.s, or we'd never have met."

"I'm glad too." There was a companionable silence, but then…

"John…," said Sara. Fisher tensed; he didn't like the sound of this.

"Ye-es?" he replied carefully.

"You know that my secondment to Marineville is only temporary, don't you?" said Sara, not looking at him.

"Yes."

"And that I'll be recalled to Washington soon."

"Yes."

"Well, I was wondering…"

"Yes?"

"Can't you say anything else, but 'Yes'?!" snapped Sara, now looking him straight in the eye.

"Ye…," Fisher just managed to stop himself.

"I was wondering too," he said instead, "if we could continue being… whatever it is we're being… even after you've gone?"

"You mean… a long-distance relationship?!" said Sara, as though the idea was completely new to her.

"Yes. Sorry. I mean… what about it?" asked Fisher hopefully.

Suddenly the computer *dinged* politely, and along the top of the machine a row of green lightbulbs flashed urgently. There was a loud *ker-lunk!* and a card was spat out into a tray on the front. Sara snatched it up, and fed it into another slot. The computer chuntered some more and then, with a loud chatter, it started to print out reams of paper that folded in zig-zags onto another tray. The printer stopped, the bell *dinged*, and the row of lights flashed again. Amazing what these new computers could do. Sara ripped off the paper read-out and leafed through it.

"I don't believe it!" she said, "They all check out."

"Even the French cook with the huge moustache?" asked Fisher, looking over her shoulder.

"Even the French cook with the huge moustache," confirmed Sara. "Chief Petty Officer Henri La Plage. Look – Orca's crew were all passed through security at Arago Point. Pictures match and everything."

Sara scrunched up the paper into a big ball, threw it towards the bin, and stormed out of the office.

"But Sara! What about... wait!" cried Fisher, and hurried after her.

Titan was feeling very pleased with how his campaign was progressing. He had the terraineans on the back foot. Without Stingray to protect them, and with the resources that his alliances with other undersea races had brought him, his victory was assured. Even now, Sculpin was overseeing the capture and conversion of more dolphins, and the artificers were rapidly completing the construction of more armoured suits. The next attack would see Marineville defeated. It was but the first step in his journey to becoming King of the entire world! Yes – he felt very pleased with himself, and so it was with only slight irritation that he accepted a voice-only call from Surface Agent X-20.

"Report!" he said peremptorily.

"Oh Despotic Titan!" said X-20 in hushed tones, but he was clearly excited, "I have some good news and some bad news."

"Well?" said Titan, stifling a yawn.

"The bad news is that the latest attack by the brass robots failed."

"I know. And the good news?"

"Ah, not yet Radiant Titan, I'm afraid there is still some more bad news! Heh-heh-heh!"

Then why was the idiot laughing in that annoying manner?

"Marineville has a new secret weapon!" continued X-20, "An advanced submarine named Orca that is bigger, faster and more fiercely be-weaponed than Stingray ever was! I am transmitting you some photographs now...".

This was grave news indeed. Titan quickly activated his wallscreen, and watched with increasing dismay as picture after picture of a large, brutish-looking vessel flashed before his eyes. The photographs were all taken at odd angles, and some were obscured by shoulders, arms and the backs of people's heads, but nothing could disguise the bulky weapons pods, the huge turbine, the sense of sheer power that emanated from the new craft.

"When were these pictures taken?" demanded Titan.

"Now we come to the good news! Heh-heh-heh!" said X-20.

"Just get on with it!" shouted Titan.

"Yes, Vigorous Titan! The good news is that the brass robot attack provided me with the diversion I needed, and I have been able to infiltrate Marineville! I took these photographs of the submarine – of Orca – this afternoon."

"And what am I supposed to do with *photographs*?"

"Oh Sublime Titan! The very best news of all is that I have an infallible plan that will deliver Orca into your hands! Soon you will be invincible!"

CHAPTER NINE

Let the Trials Begin!

Marineville had been a hive of activity overnight. The worst of the damage caused by the armoured dolphin incursion had been cleared away, and repairs quickly effected in anticipation of another attack. Meanwhile, final preparations had been made for the launch of Orca, and the beginning of her sea trials.

Admiral Stern had decided at the last minute to fly into Marineville so he could officiate at the launch, and bask in the credit for getting Project Orca completed ahead of schedule, although he'd had little to do with the actual work. He entered Submarine Pen 1 with Commander Shore hovering beside him. Captain Dune and various attendant staff followed immediately behind.

The admiral stopped involuntarily as he laid eyes on Orca for the very first time, and everyone stopped with him. Orca was raised above water level on the elevator platform, so every line of her could be appreciated. A huge blue and gold W.A.S.P. flag had been draped across her prow, and an honour guard of Marineville staff stood in ranks on the wide dockside in full dress uniform. They came to attention, the stamp of their boots deafening on the steel decking, and saluted.

"My word," said Stern, clearly awestruck, "Orca... she's quite... *formidable*, isn't she?"

"Yes, sir," said Commander Shore, "Lieutenant Sheridan calls her 'a big brute of a boat'."

"He isn't wrong. I approved all the plans, of course, but seeing her in the flesh... so to speak..." he tailed off. Captain Dune was keen to move things along and stepped forward.

"Shall we?" he said, and gestured towards a microphone stand at the edge of the dockside close to Orca's hull, where a bottle of champagne waited on a little table. Admiral Stern stepped up to the microphone and riffled through a sheaf of notes, while Commander Shore and Captain Dune took their place in the front rank of personnel where Orca's crew were waiting. From where he stood, Admiral Stern gave the crew a visual inspection. He'd read their files, obviously, but this was the first time he'd laid eyes on them, and they looked a fine body of men and women. Apart from the Chief Petty Officer on the end. That extraordinary moustache was not regulation. He'd have to have a word. But later – first he had a speech to deliver. He cleared his throat and spoke into the microphone.

"Thank you. At ease." And there was another crash of boots as the staff lowered their salutes and stood with their feet apart.

"A very good morning. It is my privilege and honour to welcome you all to the launch of the World Aquanaut Security Patrol Submarine Orca – the first of her class. She is named after the 'killer whale' – an intelligent, powerful and ruthless apex predator whose qualities are reflected in the technology, speed and weaponry of our new vessel.

"I would like to acknowledge the dedication and determination of the engineering crews, who have worked around the clock to get Orca sea-worthy in record time. You are a credit to this shipyard and to the W.A.S.P.s.

PROJECT ORCA

"The recent attacks on your home here at Marineville have demonstrated the need for a firm and decisive response to the threat posed by Titanica. Orca is that response. She has been custom-built to meet the demands of the present crisis. She has longer endurance, greater speed and more firepower than our current class of submarine. She will be the first defender of our oceans and our liberty. She will be the sword point that will strike deep into the heart of our enemies.

"We honour Captain Dirk Dune and his crew of valiant aquanauts as they commence sea trials, and wish them luck in their endeavours."

Admiral Stern put down his notes on the table beside him, and picked up the bottle of champagne by its neck.

"I name this submarine 'Orca', and give the blessing of the World Aquanaut Security Patrol to her and to all who sail in her."

Stern turned around and smashed the bottle on Orca's hull, splashing himself with foaming champagne in the process. Everyone laughed politely and applauded.

"Carry on, Captain Dune," said the admiral.

Dune and his crew stood to attention, saluted, performed a neat right turn (they'd been practising) and trooped across a metal bridge and onto Orca, while the W.A.S.P flag was pulled off her prow. Then, as buglers played an echoing fanfare, the elevator platform slowly lowered Orca into the water. With a loud whine, her huge turbine began to turn and she slowly moved off, away from the dockside, submerging completely as she went. Everyone applauded again. Commander Shore hovered his chair over to the admiral who looked down at him with a satisfied smile.

"That went rather well," said Stern, "Now let's get up to the Control Tower and observe the sea trials. I'm keen to find out if our money has been well spent."

On board Orca, Captain Dune was sitting in his new chair on the little dais at the centre of the bridge. He was drumming his fingers impatiently. The ceremony had largely been for show, and they were still at the entrance to Pen 1's launch tunnel, waiting for instructions from the Control Tower. It was all a bit of an anti-climax as far as Dune was concerned, but when he looked around at his crew, he could see that they were all on edge. The tension was palpable. But then it was the first time they'd all worked together on a brand new, untried submarine. They were bound to be feeling apprehensive. Dune pressed a button on his console to activate the ship-wide speakers.

"All crew report status. Navigation?" he said.

"All systems green, standing by for orders, sir," said Choppy Waters.

"Hydrophone?"

"Signal green. Clear as a bell, sir," said Bahari.

"Comms?"

"All channels green, sir," said Hai.

"Weapons System?"

"Fully loaded, fully charged. All systems green, sir," said Talwar.

"Engineering?"

"Like a caged dingo down here," said Beach's voice over the speaker, "Can't wait to let her rip. Green as it gets."

"And I 'ave a bouillabaisse simmering!" said La Plage's voice from the galley. "Bon voyage! Et bon appétit!"

Everyone laughed. Good, thought Dune. That had relieved the tension a little.

"Captain, I have the Tower for you," said Hai. At last!

"Tower to Orca, this is Commander Shore."

"Orca to Tower, this is Captain Dune, receiving you loud and clear."

"Sorry to keep you waiting, but I have a surprise for you."

"Oh yes?" Dune didn't like the sound of this. Shore's voice rumbled out of the speakers, failing to conceal his pleasure.

"Orca's performance today will be tested... against Stingray!"

Captain Troy Tempest and Lieutenant Phones Sheridan strode into Marineville's Standby Lounge wearing fresh silver-grey and red uniforms, complete with peaked caps bearing the W.A.S.P. crest, worn at a jaunty angle. They walked straight across the room to an alcove labelled *Injector Bay*, where they sat side by side in large ergonomic chairs.

"Okay Phones?" said Troy happily.

"You betcha, Skipper!" said his friend, and with perfect timing born of long practice, they simultaneously grabbed the levers beside their chairs and pushed them forward. The floor of the Injector Bay slid back into the wall behind them to reveal a deep shaft, and the chairs sank smoothly downwards on long poles. Troy loved this bit. They picked up speed as they descended through storey after storey until they were suddenly suspended over the chasm of Submarine Pen 3.

And there, below them, waiting on the elevator platform, was the beautiful blue, silver and gold hull of Stingray. She'd been moved here by the mechanical conveyors only an hour ago, after a very long night spent finishing her repairs. The chairs slowed their descent as they passed through Stingray's dorsal hatch, and into the bridge cockpit where they came to rest on the deck with a satisfying click. Clamps clanked shut to secure them into position, and the steering columns slid out to meet Troy and Phones. Troy gripped the familiar wheel with satisfaction, and Phones slipped his hydrophone headset on over his cap. They grinned at each other.

"Feels good to be back in action, don't it?" said Phones.

"Sure does. I just wish Marina could be with us," replied Troy. "Release injector tubes."

"Release injector tubes," said Phones. He hit a button, and the poles on which the chairs had descended quickly retracted.

"Close number one hatch," said Troy.

"Number one hatch," confirmed Phones. He pressed another button, and the dorsal hatch above their heads sealed with a clang.

"Fingers crossed. Release elevators," said Troy.

"Fingers *and* toes crossed. Release elevators," acknowledged Phones, and he pulled a lever. The whole craft shuddered briefly, and then with a loud hum, the elevator platform lowered Stingray gently into the water. Troy and Phones listened to the comforting sloshing and bubbling sounds as they sank below the surface, and winced as the hull creaked and groaned as the pressure increased. That was completely normal, Troy had to remind himself.

"Stingray to Tower," he said, "Standing by."

On Orca's bridge, the atmosphere had changed for the worse again.

"Captain Dune," said Waters, "I must object to Orca's first sea trials being turned into some sort of Sports Day. It's hardly fair play, what?"

"Relax Choppy," said Dune, "Don't you know that in the wild, orcas are known to eat stingrays for breakfast?"

"How are we…" began Waters, but Bahari, beside him at the other steering column, gave a tiny shake of the head. Waters closed his mouth with an audible *clop*.

"Lieutenant Hai, get me Stingray on the radio," said Dune with a smile.

"This is Stingray. Receiving you Orca," said Troy's voice, "What can I do for you, Captain Dune?"

"Good morning, Captain Tempest. I wondered why you weren't at the launch ceremony. Now I know. Was this your idea?"

"I believe it was Commander's Shore's. When Orca's outfitting was completed yesterday, the engineering crew volunteered to finish work on Stingray. We pulled an all-nighter to give you some healthy competition."

"Well let's make it worth the effort, shall we?"

"What do you mean?"

"I suggest a small wager," said Dune, grinning at his bridge crew. "Shall we say, a thousand dollars to whoever wins the trials?"

There was no answer from Stingray. Dune's grin widened. Then the speaker crackled.

"You're on," said Troy, and the connection was cut.

On Stingray's bridge, Phones was shaking his head sorrowfully.

"Jumpin' catfish, Skipper, are you ailing for somethin'?"

"Just imagine Dune's face when we win the bet," said Troy with unconvincing bravado.

"Tower to Stingray," said Atlanta's voice, "You are clear for launch."

"Stingray to Tower. P.W.O.R!" replied Troy, and then to Phones he said, "Acceleration Rate One."

"Acceleration Rate One."

The huge oval door of Pen 3 slid open, and Stingray's sleek fish-shaped body slipped gracefully through and into the launch tunnel beyond, the whine of her turbine rising in pitch as she reached 100 knots on the 10-mile approach to the ocean door, which was already grinding open ahead of them.

The tunnel's mouth was set into the sheer face of an undersea cliff, and with an effervescent gush of bubbles, Stingray shot out like a cork popping out of a champagne bottle.

Almost simultaneously, a few hundred yards down the coast, another, much wider ocean door slid open in the undersea cliffs, and Orca's broad prow punched through like a barbed arrowhead, out into the Pacific Ocean.

"Stingray and Orca seaborne," reported Atlanta.

Admiral Stern was standing beside Commander Shore at the Control Tower tracking station, and they watched as the two submarines appeared as blips on the big circular screen.

"This *is* exciting," said Stern, "What's on the programme for this afternoon?" What did he think this was? A day at the races?

"We have three trials arranged," said Shore, "designed to test manoeuvrability, weaponry and speed." He lifted his microphone.

"Tower to Orca and Stingray. Here are your instructions. You are to proceed to the W.A.S.P. missile range at west-north-west 1300, reference Z. On the way, a zig-zag course will be dictated by a series of signal beacons, and you must pass within twenty feet of each one to activate the beacon's proximity alarm, or you will be disqualified. This is both a race, and a test of your ship's manoeuvrability, so be on the lookout for obstacles along the way, and watch your speed. The beacons will begin transmitting on my mark. Are you ready?"

"Orca to Tower. We're ready, P.W.O.R," said Captain Dune.

"Stingray to Tower. We're ready, P.W.O.R," said Captain Tempest.

Shore looked at Fisher who nodded, and then spoke again into his microphone.

"Three, two, one, *mark!*"

And Fisher threw a switch to activate the signal beacons. The sea trials had begun.

CHAPTER TEN

Stingray for Breakfast?

Orca took an early lead, with Stingray trailing in her wake. On Orca's bridge, Dune was leaning forward in his seat, smiling with satisfaction.

"It's a straight dash to the first beacon, but the second is behind us to starboard," said Bahari.

"I say! Recommend lowering our speed a tad or we'll overshoot the turn, what?" said Waters.

"Keep her at Rate Five," said Dune.

"But, sir...," persisted Waters.

"Rate Five!" shouted Dune.

"Aye-aye, sir."

On Stingray, Troy and Phones were both frowning with concentration.

"Here's where experience counts," said Troy. "Keep her at Rate Four."

"Rate Four," confirmed Phones. He put a hand to his right hydrophone speaker and pressed it closer to his ear.

"First beacon coming up..." he said.

"As soon as the proximity alarm pings..."

"Now!"

"Green one-twenty!" said Troy, and Stingray performed a sharp turn around the beacon to head straight for the second.

"Nice," said Phones, putting a hand back to his ear, "and we just left Orca behind!"

"Green one-twenty! Green one-twenty!" Dune was yelling. Waters and Bahari were sweating as they fought with the helm controls, but eventually Orca turned in a wide arc onto the new course.

"May I recommend...," began Waters.

"No, you may not!" snapped Dune.

Admiral Stern and Commander Shore were following the trial's progress at the tracking station.

"Schoolboy error," said Stern.

"Rookie mistake," agreed Shore. "Let's hope Captain Dune learns from it. There's another sharp turn coming up."

"Red one-ten!" said Troy, and Stingray performed a perfect turn around the second beacon, finishing with a flamboyant barrel roll to head for the third.

"Red one-ten, red one-ten!" yelled Dune, as Orca screamed past the beacon, then pulled around in another long, laborious curve.

In the Control Tower, Admiral Stern shook his head sadly.

"Stingray's making Orca look like a tugboat so far. Very disappointing." Shore tried hard not to look smug.

"I think the problem is human error, sir. But they'd better start thinking ahead because the course is about to take them through Neptune's Fingers."

Stingray slipped past the third beacon and suddenly, huge pillars of rock loomed out of the deep-sea murk ahead of them, like a forest of blackened tree-trunks after a fire.

"Neptune's Fingers!" exclaimed Phones, "The fourth beacon is plumb in the middle of them!"

"Reduce speed to Rate Two!" said Troy.

"Rate Two!"

"Red seven-five!... Green three-five!... Red nine-oh!" And Stingray slalomed elegantly between the rocks, pinging the fourth beacon as she went.

"Reduce speed! Reduce speed!" screamed Dune, standing up on his little dais and waving his arms, as the massive pillars appeared from the gloom.

"Rate Two!" ordered Waters.

"Rate Two!" confirmed Bahari.

"Red six... no, seven-five...!" said Dune, sitting back down. Waters' eyes widened even further behind his horn-rimmed glasses, and he looked across at Bahari, and was relieved to see that — for all their sakes — the helmsman had taken the split-second decision to steer the ship through Neptune's Fingers without the Captain's advice. Orca twisted and wove, her bulk suddenly dancing lightly through the rocks with agile precision.

"That's more like it!" exclaimed Admiral Stern, watching the screen.

"One more surprise to go!" said Shore.

Stingray shot out from between the last of Neptune's Fingers, heading for the fifth beacon.

"Looks like a straight line to the missile range!" said Phones, "Let's pour it on!"

"Rate Four only, Phones. Keep your wits about you. Remember — this is a test of manoeuvrability!"

"You got it, Skipper. Rate Four."

Orca came corkscrewing out of the forest of rocks, and steadied on her keel as she headed off in pursuit.

"Excellent teamwork!" said Dune, "We can't be far behind Stingray now. Rate Six!"

"Rate Six," confirmed Waters.

Phones frowned as he listened to the aural landscape in his headset.

"The next beacon's coming up dead ahead... but it's almost like... Troy! There's a cliff face beyond it! We're headed straight for it!"

"Cut engine," said Troy calmly.

Stingray continued under her own momentum as the dark underwater cliff appeared ahead and above, but there was the beacon! And its proximity alarm pinged. Stingray's engine powered up again and her prow lifted until she was almost vertical.

"Acceleration Rate One; blow tanks 1 and 3!" said Troy.

Stingray rose effortlessly in a cloud of bubbles to the top of the cliff where she levelled out over a wide undersea plateau.

"Missile range dead ahead," said Troy, "Rate Four!"

"Pull up! Pull up! Pull up!" screamed Bahari as the cliff face echoed its hard, uncompromising signal back into his hydrophones. He and Waters pulled back on their control columns as hard as they could, and Orca powered up the cliff, the curve of the vessel's trajectory taking her closer and closer to the rock face. The bridge crew all watched with frozen expressions of horror as the dark wall rushed downwards in front of the cockpit windows. Closer, closer, closer... then the hard line of the cliff top appeared.

Orca's belly clipped the edge as she cleared it, sending shards of rock spinning away in underwater slow-motion.

Dune released the white-knuckled grip he'd had on the arms of his chair, and thumbed the intercom button.

"Damage report!" he said.

"Fair dinkum, sir," replied Beach over the speaker, "She's built to last!"

"But I 'ave bouillabaisse all over zer ceiling!" added La Plage from the galley.

"We can still catch Stingray!" said Dune, clenching his fist, "I won't be beaten by Troy Tempest! Rate Six!"

"Orca was built using a new alloy we salvaged from an enemy craft," Shore was explaining to the Admiral, "She's virtually indestructible!"

"Even so," said Stern, "I would prefer not to put it to the test again."

"They're approaching the finish line now, sir."

Stingray streaked towards the final beacon, but suddenly, Orca appeared behind her, and she was gaining fast.

Troy decided to throw caution to the wind.

"Rate Six!" he ordered as Orca passed the port windows.

"Too late, Skipper!" said Phones. The beacon pinged in his ears, "That's it!... the race is over."

Back in Marineville, Commander Shore raised his microphone.

"Tower to Orca and Stingray. The first trial is over. Orca passed the finish line a second before Stingray. But she failed to set off the proximity alarm on Beacon Five before the cliff. Stingray is therefore the victor of the manoeuvrability trial. Congratulations Captain Tempest. The second trial will test the weaponry of your ships. You will each have three moving targets to destroy as quickly as you can. Stingray – as the present leader, you will go first."

"Tower from Stingray, standing by," came Troy's voice over the speaker, sounding very confident.

"Stingray from Tower," said Shore, "you can expect your three targets any time... now!" and he flicked a switch.

"P.W.O.R!" replied Troy.

At the far side of the W.A.S.P. missile range, a huge target appeared out of an undersea cave, travelling along a rail. It was a life-sized representation of a mechanical fish, the type of submarine used by Titan's Aquaphibian forces. It was shaped a little like a deep-sea angler fish, with a broad, powerful body covered in armoured scales, a wide mouth that housed missile tubes, and two bulbous eyes for windows. Privately, the W.A.S.P personnel called them Terror Fish. Fortunately, this was only a two-dimensional target, but as it picked up speed along the rail, it was soon travelling faster than the real thing. And from the cave mouth behind it, two more of the Terror Fish targets emerged.

On Stingray's bridge, Troy and Phones were still flushed with their success in the first trial.

"Sting missiles armed and ready," announced Troy, "Let's show Orca some sharp shooting!"

Phones smiled as he listened to the signals in his headset.

"First target approaching, Skipper!" he reported.

"Point me at it!" said Troy.

"Here she comes... wait for it... Green four-two!"

"Green four-two!" acknowledged Troy.

Stingray swooped towards the target, which was approaching fast to starboard. A Sting missile whooshed from Stingray's prow and hit the Terror Fish dead centre. It exploded in a satisfying ball of broiling smoke and flame. Stingray pulled up and away to avoid the debris, and looped around in pursuit of the two other targets. They were already speeding away across the range, disappearing and reappearing as they flashed between the rocks.

Stingray launched another Sting missile which cut a straight white trail through the water and hit the second target, destroying it completely. But the third target sped on, and Stingray had to peel off to avoid a rocky outcrop. She performed a neat spiralling turn and came around to get the Terror Fish back in her sights. It was at extreme range now, and if the final target reached the far side of the range, the trial would be over. Another Sting missile streaked away from Stingray's prow... and kept going... and kept going... then...

BOOM!

...the target was scattered all over the ocean floor.

"Impressive," said Admiral Stern checking the Control Tower's instruments, "All three targets destroyed in four minutes and twenty seconds. Let's see if Orca can do any better."

"Orca from Tower," said Shore, "are you ready?"

"Tower from Orca, standing by," said Dune's voice.

"You can expect your three targets any time... now!" and Shore flicked the switch.

"P.W.O.R!" replied Dune.

Captain Dirk Dune swivelled in his chair to face the Weapons Station, a cold, steely look of determination in his blue eyes.

"Lieutenant Talwar?" he said.

"Killer missiles armed, ray guns charged, sonic cannon primed," answered Talwar with a smile.

"Then let's not mess about," said Dune, "it's time to show them what a real battleship can do."

Orca powered towards the first Terror Fish target as it sped across the range. A Killer missile roared away from one of her four bow tubes, and she was already turning towards the second target when the first was atomised by a huge, dazzlingly bright explosion. The water boiled away in oily waves, leaving nothing of the Terror Fish.

The second target had disappeared behind some rocks, but Orca's weapons system had its trajectory and the sonic cannon throbbed a deep pulse of infrasound that rippled out through the water in a cone of expanding concentric circles. The rocks and the target passing behind them were blasted into powder. Orca soared upwards and backwards, rolling to turn right side up, and then dived towards the third target.

Thin, red lines of bright light shot out from the ray guns beneath her fins to port and starboard. The beams danced back and forth, up and down, all over the target, slicing and dicing the final Terror Fish into tiny squares of confetti that floated gently away across the range.

"Good grief!" exclaimed Admiral Stern. Then he let out a loud, unattractive bark of laughter. "Hah! All three targets destroyed – no *obliterated!* – in just fifty-seven seconds!"

"Orca certainly is an awesome weapon," agreed Shore, but he didn't sound pleased at all. He raised his microphone again.

"Tower to Orca and Stingray. The second trial is over. Orca wins. The third and final trial will be a flat race back to base. No obstacles this time – your course back to the first beacon is unobstructed. Let's see how fast you are."

"Orca to Tower. We're ready, P.W.O.R," acknowledged Captain Dune over the speaker.

"Stingray to Tower. We're ready, P.W.O.R," acknowledged Captain Tempest.

"Then on my mark," said Shore, "Three, two, one, mark!"

Orca and Stingray powered away from the Missile Range, heading in a straight line for the coast. Stingray was quicker off the mark, and powered ahead of Orca, leaving the larger vessel in her bubbling wake.

"Come on Phones!" said Troy, "We can do this. We can't let Dune beat us."

"We're doing 450 knots, still accelerating," said Phones, "Orca's behind us but matching us for speed."

"Come on Choppy," said Dune, "We can do this. We can't let Tempest beat us."

"We're doing 500 knots, still accelerating," said Choppy.

"Beginning to gain on Stingray," said Bahari. Dune leaned forward in his seat, his eyes peering through the front windows. He thumbed the intercom.

"Beach, I need everything you can give me," he said.

"You're getting it, Captain," replied Beach from the engine room, "She's going flat out."

"Rate Six!" announced Choppy excitedly, "We're doing 600 knots and still accelerating!"

"And there she is!" said Dune with satisfaction, as Stingray's wake re-appeared ahead of them.

"Rate Six point Five!" cried Choppy.

"Orca coming up alongside, Skipper!" said Phones, and Orca appeared in the port windows again, passing them with apparent ease.

"Come on, Stingray!" yelled Troy, and rammed the throttle lever as far forward as it would go. There was a loud bang, and clouds of black, acrid smoke filled the bridge.

"Not again!" wailed Troy, "Not now!"

Phones was already out of his seat and aiming a fire extinguisher at the blown-out panel. The noise of Stingray's engine was decreasing rapidly in pitch as they decelerated, and Troy flapped the smoke away from his eyes to watch through the front windows as Orca's massive turbine churned away into the distance.

"Orca not only wins the sea trials," said Admiral Stern with satisfaction, "but also sets a new speed record. 652 knots!"

Shore didn't reply. He hovered his chair along the central console until he was beside Atlanta.

"Sorry honey," he said quietly, "You'd better send a rescue launch out to tow Stingray home. Again."

CHAPTER ELEVEN

Shakedown

That evening, the Blue Lagoon – Marineville's best (and only) restaurant – rang with the sound of boisterous revelry as Captain Dirk Dune celebrated Orca's victory with his crew.

"...and the best thing is," said Dune, coming to the end of his speech, "Captain Tempest now owes me a thousand dollars!"

Everyone cheered and brayed with laughter. But then Dune waved them quiet, and chose his most serious expression. He put his empty glass down on the bar and resumed his speech.

"I'm sorry to finish on a serious note, but it has to be said. I think we'd all agree that some of us – mentioning no names – could have performed a little better out there today. There were times when I was carrying you. Taking up the slack. Covering for your mistakes." He looked at each one of his crew in turn. "So get a good night's sleep, because tomorrow you'll report to Pen 1 at oh-eight-hundred hours and we will embark upon a shakedown cruise to iron out the kinks, deal with the teething problems, oil the wheels and get us all working smoothly together as a team."

Dune had expected sullen silence or, at best, disgruntled agreement, so he was surprised to receive a round of applause, enthusiastically led by his second-in-command.

"Capital idea!" said Choppy, "Couldn't agree with you more, old chap!"

The applause died away, and the crew quickly finished their drinks and began to head for the door. Choppy sidled up to Dune.

"I'm assuming we'll be alone on this shakedown-whatnot?" he said, "No Stingray to keep an eye on us this time?"

"No Choppy," said Dune, "It'll be just Orca, us, and the wide blue ocean. I think we've all seen the last of Stingray."

"I don't understand it," said Phones, "I checked and double-checked the engines myself."

"Then why do we keep getting the feedback problem?" said Troy. "It's just as well these fuses blew again, or the whole thing could have gone up."

Stingray had been returned to Pen 3 where Troy and Phones were assessing the damage.

"Beats me," sighed Phones, "I'll finish changing all these fuses, and then head back down to the engine room. Check, double check and triple check this time." He got no answer. "Skipper?"

"That's it. I've had it up to here," said Troy angrily, "Putting Marina under house arrest, taking Atlanta out on dates, insulting Stingray, winning the bet!" He slammed down his wrench and stamped away towards the aft hatch.

"Where're you headed, Troy?"

"To do something about Dirk Dune and his precious Orca!"

Marina was bored out of her mind. She'd watched all her favourite Johnny Swoonara videofilms, listened to all her favourite Duke Dexter records, tidied all her cupboards, and arranged all her books in alphabetical order. Now she was lying on her sofa, listlessly turning the pages of a magazine, aching to be back at sea where she belonged.

Sara and Atlanta had both dropped in a couple of times, but they were very busy with their duties. She'd seen nothing of Troy or Phones but didn't expect to, what with... hang on. She turned her head to listen. That sounded like Troy now, speaking to the guard outside. There was a knock on the door, and Marina ran to open it, but her smile of welcome faded when she saw the grim expression on Troy's face.

"Hey Marina," he said, "How are you? Mind if I sit down for a minute?" Marina shook her head – of course not! Troy slumped into an armchair, and Marina gestured towards the drinks trolley that she kept well-stocked for when Phones or Commander Shore paid a visit.

"No thanks," said Troy, "I just wanted to talk some things over with you."

Marina sat opposite him and raised a mocking eyebrow.

"Yeah, 'spose I'll do all the talking. Sorry. But talking to you always makes me feel calmer. And everything's been so crazy recently. Ever since Dirk Dune turned up."

Marina frowned and made a dismissive gesture – she didn't care about Dirk Dune.

"But because of Dune, you're locked up in your own apartment, Phones is scrabbling around for parts to repair Stingray and I'm a thousand dollars poorer."

Marina cocked her head.

"Never mind about that," Troy went on hurriedly, "I just wanted to tell you that I'm going to put this right."

The next morning, Lieutenant Sara Coral was immensely pleased to find out that Orca had launched with all her crew aboard. With them safely out at sea, she could do some more checking up. Even though the computer had seemed happy that the crew were who they said they were, something about them was still bothering her. Nothing she could put her finger on. She had no reason to suspect them. Except maybe the Frenchman's extraordinary moustache, but having extravagant facial hair that *might* be a disguise wouldn't be enough to convince Commander Shore that Henri La Plage was a spy. Not on its own, anyway. Sara needed proof, and she was on her way to the crew's accommodation block to find it. Strictly speaking, she was bending the rules, but if she found the evidence she was looking for…

Henri La Plage's quarters were the obvious place to start. She unlocked the door with her pass key, checked to make sure she was unobserved, and slipped inside closing the door behind her. The place was a mess. It looked like there had been a fight. A chair was overturned, a vase had been smashed, a picture was askew, a rug was rumpled. Sara stepped further into the room, her eyes taking in every detail. Not only had there been a fight, but someone had been searching for something as well. The wardrobe doors were hanging open, and a suitcase lay unzipped on the bed, its contents spread out all over the floor.

Sara raised her arm to speak into her wrist radio, but… what was that? She'd heard something. Coming from the bathroom. And there it was again – a low groan. Someone was in there. Sara drew her pistol from its holster.

"Hello? This is Lieutenant Coral, Head of Security! I'm armed!"

She nudged the bathroom door with her foot, and it creaked open. A man was lying fully clothed in the empty bath, tied up and gagged with torn strips of bedsheet. It was Henri La Plage! Sara holstered her pistol, knelt down beside him and removed the gag.

"Chief La Plage? Are you okay?" she said. La Plage opened his eyes, saw Sara and emitted a little shriek.

"Zut alors! Tied me up! Dumped me in zer bath! Stole ma spare uniform!" he spluttered.

"You mean... someone's taken your place on Orca?!" Sara stood up and spoke urgently into her wrist radio. "Coral to Tower..."

At that moment, Orca was cruising along at a modest Rate Four, following a pre-arranged patrol course that would take her far out across the Pacific Ocean. Apart from the constant low hum of the powerful engines, all was quiet on the bridge. Dune had made himself comfortable in the captain's chair, and was lying back with a leg over one of the arms, taking stock of his life. He had a cool submarine, he had a crew who clearly idolised him, and he was on the fast track to becoming an admiral. Yeah – he was feeling pretty good this morning, despite a slight hangover. But he could do something about that. He thumbed the intercom switch and spoke to the galley.

"La Plage! A cup of Earl Grey tea at your earliest convenience!" he said. There was no reply.

"Chief! Respondez, s'il vous plait!" he said and tried to catch Talwar's eye to share the joke, but she continued to stare at her console.

"Er... oui," said a small voice over the speaker.

"Our Gallic friend seems unusually quiet this morning," said Dune, "Too many glasses of vin rouge last night maybe!" No one laughed. They all seemed preoccupied. Concentrating on the job! Excellent! He was whipping them into shape already!

In the galley, an imposter wearing chef's whites and disguised with an extravagantly curled false moustache was searching frantically through the various cupboards for teabags. Then he stopped. What was he doing? He daren't take a cup of tea up to Captain Dune. The disguise had been sufficient to get him on board Orca, but he doubted it would bear close inspection on the bridge. Maybe now was the time to put his plan into action?

In the Control Tower, Commander Shore was listening with growing concern to Lieutenant Coral's voice as she radio-ed in her report.

"So it looks like one of Titan's Surface Agents has somehow infiltrated Marineville and disguised himself as Chief La Plage. He's presumably on board Orca right now," Sara concluded.

"Thank you, Lieutenant," said Shore. "Look after La Plage, and see if you can get any more out of him, regarding our intruder and his plans."

"P.W.O.R!" replied Sara.

Shore ended the call, and spun his hoverchair around to face his daughter.

"Radio Orca at once!" he barked. "Let them know they have a stowaway on board!"

Atlanta nodded and spoke into her microphone.

"Orca from Tower, Orca from Tower, come in please," but she only received a hiss of static in reply. She looked at her father.

"Keep trying," he ordered, "There's no need to panic just yet."

But Atlanta could tell he was worried.

Sara finished her call to the Tower, closed her wrist radio, and knelt back down beside the bath to start untying Henri La Plage.

"If there's anything you can tell me about the person who did this to you, it could be helpful," she said.

"Non, non, I 'ave no idea oo 'ee was," shrugged La Plage, "'Ee was wearing a disguise. A big moustache like mine."

"He? So it was definitely a..." Sara suddenly stopped working at the knots around the man's wrists. Where the strips of bed linen had rubbed against his skin, there were traces of make-up. Flesh coloured make-up. She picked up the gag she had already removed from around his head and examined it. More flesh-coloured smudges. Sara looked closely at the man's face. It was covered in a thick layer of flesh-coloured greasepaint, but there were patches where the gag had smeared it, and the man's natural skin tone could be seen beneath. And he was green. With a feeling of immense vindication, Sara ripped off the huge false moustache.

"Ow!" said the man, "Flippin' eck! Wotchoo do that for?!"

What was that accent? Sara got to her feet, leaving him still tied up and helpless in the bath. He began to panic.

"Hey! What's goin' on?! Untie me! I fought you wanted to know about the bloke what stole my clothes!"

"Did he steal your French accent too?" said Sara, smiling down at him.

"Oh, I... you know: I'm a chef. Sort of expected. Got stuck wiv it..." gabbled the man.

"But if you're here, who took your place on Orca? This doesn't make any sense."

"I'm the victim here! Aren't you going to help me?"

"Nope. I'm arresting you," said Sara with satisfaction, "You're charged with espionage and impersonating a Frenchman. Badly."

There was a tense atmosphere in the Control Tower. Orca had missed a scheduled check-in, altered course, and then disappeared altogether from the scopes. Then Lieutenant Coral had radio-ed in again to explain that the man in the bath wasn't Henri La Plage after all – he was a Titanican agent. Did that mean that the real La Plage was safely on

Orca? Coral had checked the rooms of Orca's other crew members, and they were empty, so it looked like there'd only been one attempt at substitution, and that had been foiled. Or had it? Because Orca had disappeared. So maybe there were two agents at work? What in thunder was going on?

Commander Shore hovered his chair over to Fisher who was staring at the blank tracking screen.

"See if you can boost the power," said Shore, "but if Orca's Camouflage System has been activated, I doubt it will make any difference."

"I'll give it my best shot, sir!" replied Fisher. Shore gave him a grim smile and hovered back towards the central console where Atlanta was still trying to raise Orca on the radio.

"Orca from Tower, Orca from Tower, come in please." She turned to her father. "No reply. Are we sure she's been hijacked? There might have been a terrible accident, or an attack from Titanica!"

"I don't know," admitted Shore, "but it's got to have something to do with the mystery man that Lieutenant Coral found tied up in La Plage's bath!" How was he going to break the news to Admiral Stern that they'd lost his brand new, state-of-the-art, armed-to-the-teeth, extremely expensive submarine, only a day after her launch? At least the Admiral had flown back to Washington. Didn't have to face him just yet.

"Shouldn't we launch Stingray?" asked Atlanta, breaking into his thoughts.

"No can do, honey – she's still being repaired."

Shore came to a decision.

"Call Action Stations," he ordered, "and scramble Air Support. The only thing we can do is search Orca's last known co-ordinates."

"P.W.O.R!" said Atlanta. She pressed a button and the Action Stations drumbeat sounded out across Marineville.

"Air Support from Tower..." she said into her microphone.

As Atlanta relayed the Commander's instructions, Sara exited the elevator and strode into the room, looking more than usually determined.

"Any updates?" said Shore, spinning his chair to face her. Sara took a deep breath and began her report.

"The man in the bath is definitely not Henri La Plage. He's a Titanican Surface Agent code-named G-66, but that's all he'll tell us. I've been in touch with the W.A.S.P. Mediterranean base in Toulon, and they're sure it was the real La Plage who left France a few days ago. And apparently, he really does have a huge moustache. So the substitution can only have happened at Arago Point, before he even got to Marineville. The Security Team there is already looking into it, but I'd like to fly over to Arago Airbase myself and follow my line of enquiry. With your permission, of course."

"Granted," said Shore, "But Lieutenant, if the real La Plage never made it to Marineville, and the Titanican substitute's plan was to infiltrate Orca's crew and stage a hijack..."

"...then how did he end up in the bath, who took his place and what's happened to Orca?" completed Sara.

CHAPTER TWELVE

The Stowaway

Captain Dirk Dune surfaced from a light snooze with a little snort. He glanced quickly around Orca's bridge to see if any of the crew had noticed, but they were all quietly preoccupied at their separate stations. Good. But where was his cup of tea? It had never arrived.

Dune was just about to call the galley again when he saw a light blinking on his console. What did that mean? He sat up and pushed a few buttons.

"Watch your heading, Choppy. Looks like we've drifted off course," he said. But Waters made no acknowledgement, and continued to look straight ahead out of the front windows.

"Lieutenant Bahari?" tried Dune, "Why the course change?" No answer. No sign that Bahari had even heard him. Dune was about to administer a stinging rebuke, when he saw another light flashing on his console. Now what?

"Look sharp, Lieutenant Hai," he said, "Marineville Tower is trying to contact us." No response. Dune began to feel uneasy. He giggled nervously.

"What is this? A mutiny?" he said with forced good humour. Still not a word from the crew. Then someone started to laugh. It was an unpleasant, high-pitched, mean cackle, and it took Dune a moment to realise that it was coming from his second-in-command.

"Choppy?... Lieutenant Commander Waters?" said Dune, his voice wavering. Choppy stood and turned to face him, drawing his sidearm.

"Talwar! Hai!" yelled Dune, but the Lieutenants also turned and aimed their pistols at him. Talwar stepped forward and relieved Dune of his weapon. Only Bahari remained in his seat, steering Orca to who knew where.

"Heh-heh-heh! I am not Lieutenant Commander Christopher Waters," said Choppy in a nasal voice, quite unlike his usual English pomp. "The last attack on Marineville by the armoured dolphins was precisely timed to coincide with the arrival of your new crew."

"You all had to be diverted to Arago Point," said Dune, still unsure where this was going.

"Where they remain, allowing us to take their place," continued the man who wasn't Choppy.

"Then... who are you?" said Dune.

"I am X-20, Surface Agent of the Prodigious Titan!" and Dune watched agog as the man peeled off his neat moustache and flicked it onto the floor. Then he pulled off his wig of wavy brown hair to uncover a head of short, oily, blue-green tufts. Next, he took off the horn-rimmed glasses, and Dune was surprised to see that the wide staring eyes remained wide and staring. It wasn't the lenses – that was actually what his eyes looked like. Finally, the man produced a handkerchief with a flourish, and began to wipe the make-up off his face to reveal silvery-green skin beneath.

"You mean... you're all Titanican agents? The whole crew?" said Dune.

"The whole crew!" said the creature. Disguise removed, he stepped towards Dune who cringed backwards into his chair. X-20 pressed the intercom button to speak to his fellow agents below decks.

The man with the extravagantly curly false moustache was creeping along the corridor away from the galley. The walls were bare metal, and colour-coded pipes and trunking hung in a thick cluster from the ceiling, snaking overhead along the length of the passageway. Clearly, not much thought had been given to Orca's interior decor. The PA speaker blipped and an unpleasant, nasal voice made an announcement.

"This is X-20! Our plan has succeeded! Captain Dune has been relieved of command and Orca is now in Titanican hands!"

The man with the false moustache stopped and stared at the PA speaker in astonishment. Then he reached for his sidearm, but of course! He was dressed as a chef, and wasn't wearing his holster. He walked quickly back to the galley, selected a large frying pan and gave it an experimental swing.

X-20 was enjoying himself immensely.

"Talwar and Hai... I mean Agent H-27 and Agent C-101, tie up the captain and lock him in his cabin."

"Yes X-20," chorused the Surface Agents, and they each grabbed one of Dune's arms and dragged him towards the companionway to take him below.

"When Admiral Stern hears about this..." yelled Dune and then realised he didn't know what Admiral Stern would do. What *could* he do? The situation was hopeless. "You'll be sorry!" he finished weakly. X-20 cackled adenoidally, and turned to the man who wasn't Bahari.

"Agent K-33! Set course for the rendezvous! Rate Four. Heh-heh-heh! We will present our prize to the Avaricious Titan, and the final phase of his plan can commence!" And at last, he thought to himself, he might get a bit of respect.

Because he'd pulled it off. He'd actually gone and pulled it off. The hijack plan was a success! Titan had not been pleased by the delay of twenty-four hours, but Stingray's unexpected presence at the sea trials yesterday had made a hijack attempt far too risky. Today though, everything had gone by the numbers. In fact, they were running ahead of schedule, so there was no need to hurry, and he could relax for a bit. With Orca's Camouflage System activated, there was no way the W.A.S.P.s would ever find them, and at Rate Four, they would be in plenty of time for their mid-ocean rendezvous with the Warmongering Titan and his indomitable armada of mechanical fish. Then Marineville would fall before the combined might of the undersea races!

Marina could hear the Action Stations signal from her apartment, and was beginning to fret. What was going on? She went to the window, and was just in time to see a squadron of W.A.S.P. Arrowhead Interceptor jets scream overhead. Was there going to be another attack? What would happen to those poor dolphins? She was relieved to hear a knock at her door, and rushed to open it.

"Hey Marina," said Sara, "Can I come in?"

Marina nodded and gestured to a chair, but Sara remained standing.

"Sorry, can't stop. I just wanted to let you know that I won't be around for a bit. I've got to fly over to Arago Airbase today."

Marina pointed out of the window at the loudspeakers on the street and tilted her head questioningly.

"Why has Action Stations been called?" guessed Sara. Marina nodded.

"I probably shouldn't tell you this, but Orca has disappeared. It's all very confusing – we think she might have been hijacked but..." Sara stopped talking because Marina had suddenly gone very pale and was wringing her hands anxiously.

"What's wrong?" asked Sara. Marina darted across the room to her sideboard and picked up a framed photograph of Troy. She thrust it towards Sara.

"Troy? What about him?" But then her wrist radio buzzed.

"Coral from Tower, this is Commander Shore."

"This is Coral, go ahead, sir."

"We've just had a call from Arago Airbase. They've found Orca's crew. All of them. Alive but tied up and locked in an outbuilding."

"Which means our first hunch was correct, sir. Orca is in Titanican hands."

"Looks that way. The imposters somehow managed to meet each member of the crew as they got off their separate planes and helicopters. By the time they went through security screening, the substitutions had already taken place. Get over to Arago Point and see if the crew can tell you anything useful about their doppelgangers."

"Yes, sir."

"And while you're there, explain to the Airbase staff what the word 'security' actually means."

Sara smiled.

"P.W.O.R." She closed her wrist radio and turned to Marina, who was now pointing urgently at Troy's photo.

"I'm really sorry, Marina, but I've got to go." Sara backed away towards the door. "Troy's working on Stingray with Phones. They'll be back out there as soon as they can. Don't worry." With an apologetic smile, Sara walked out of the door, and it closed in Marina's face.

Agent K-33 was still at Orca's helm, H-27 was back at the Weapons Station, and C-101 was at Comms. X-20 had made himself comfortable in the captain's chair, and was taking stock of his life. He had just captured the world's most advanced submarine, he had a crew who respected him, and he was – at long last – going to take his rightful place, high up in Titan's court. Chancellor perhaps, or Keeper of the Shrine of Teufel. How hard could that be? Yes – he was feeling pretty good this morning. But he knew what would make him feel even better. He pressed the intercom button and spoke to the galley.

"La Plage! I mean, G-66! A cup of seaweed tea at your earliest convenience!" he said and winked at H-27. She looked away quickly. There was no response from the galley.

"G-66! A cup of seaweed tea, please. And a biscuit." X-20 waited... still nothing. He stabbed at the intercom button a few times and tried again.

"Hello? G-66?"

Silence.

"Hai... I mean C-101, get down to the galley and see if there's a problem with the intercom," he said, and was gratified when the agent nodded deferentially and left the bridge without another word. X-20 smiled. He could get used to this.

Agent C-101, alias Lieutenant Hai, made his way down to the middle deck and walked along the narrow corridor towards Orca's galley.

"G-66? You there?" he called, "Our new Lord and Master wants his cup of tea! Just our luck, eh? We get rid of one narcissist, only for another to take his place."

He rounded the corner into the galley to be confronted by a man wielding a large frying pan.

"G-66?" said Hai, but he wasn't sure. The man reached up with his free hand, and peeled off his curly moustache.

"Troy Tempest!" gasped Hai, and reached for his gun.

BONNNG!

The frying pan made a satisfying noise as it bounced off C-101's head. His eyes rolled upwards and he collapsed in an undignified heap on the floor.

"One down, four to go," said Troy to himself, "and now I have a gun." He bent down to undo the agent's holster.

On the bridge, X-20 was getting impatient. He jabbed his intercom button again.

"G-66? Are you there? C-101? What's going on? Can anyone hear me?"

"Hearing you loud and clear," said Agent S-303's voice from the engine room, "Is there a problem?"

"No, no. No problem. I just wanted a cup of tea, that's all."

Troy climbed down the companionway ladder to the third and lowest deck, and tiptoed aft towards the engine room. He peered around the edge of the bulkhead door and could see Sandy Beach, or whoever she really was, tinkering at an inspection panel with her back to him, an open toolbox at her feet. Beyond her, the huge red cylinders that housed Orca's nuclear reactor towered up through all three decks. Troy stepped into the room and aimed his pistol.

"Hands up!" he shouted over the noise of the engine. Beach froze, then slowly raised her arms. Troy walked towards her, his finger tight on the gun's trigger.

"Turn around!" he called. Beach performed a mocking pirouette to face him, and smiled warmly.

"G-day Captain Tempest," she said, and nodded towards his gun, "What's got you all riled up?"

"You can drop the act. I know you're one of Titan's agents."

"And you're here to arrest me, is that it?"

"That's right."

"And how are you going to do that?" Beach's smile widened, "Because you can't go firing that thing in here," she nodded at Troy's gun again. "One stray shot and boom! We all go up together." She lowered her arms. The smile disappeared and she stooped to pick up a wrench. This wasn't quite how Troy had imagined this going. He regretted not bringing the frying pan.

"Do the sensible thing..." he began, but Beach suddenly lunged forwards, and swung at him with the wrench. Troy jerked his head backwards, and felt the wrench brush past the end of his nose. He took a step backwards towards the door and looked around for a weapon, but Beach came at him again, and he was driven further and further back as the wrench swiped viciously through the air, back and forth, closer and closer. Troy thought quickly. Could he risk a shot? What would happen if he did hit the reactor? What sort of emergency systems did Orca have?

Troy skipped backwards out of harm's way, through the doorway and into the passage. Beach grinned maniacally at him and brandished the wrench, ready to charge. Troy hit a big red button and a heavy bulkhead door slammed down between them, sealing the room with Beach still inside. Troy watched through the thick glass of a tiny porthole as white plumes of gas shot from pipes all along the walls to fill the engine room with a thick mist. Beach mouthed something at Troy through the window, and then slid downwards out of sight.

"Good night, sleep tight," said Troy. He suddenly wished Phones was with him. He'd have enjoyed that. Troy had activated the fire suppression system, which sealed the room and filled it with carbon dioxide. He hit a big green button and watched through the porthole as the gas was vented. Then the door slid upwards to reveal Beach, unconscious on the floor. She'd have a doozy of a headache when she woke up.

"Two down, three to go," mused Troy. "Might be time to enlist some help."

A red light was blinking on X-20's console.

"There's a fire in the engine room!" he wailed. Talwar rushed across the bridge to the Comms Station and checked the dials and screens.

"False alarm!" she said, "None of the smoke alarms or heat sensors have been tripped. There must have been a malfunction in the fire suppression system."

X-20 stabbed the intercom button.

"Beach! Agent S-303! Report! What's going on down there?"

But there was no answer.

"I think we've got a loose cannon on deck," said Talwar, "Maybe Captain Dune has managed to get out of his cabin?"

"Or it could just be some crossed wires," suggested Bahari mildly. "No intercom, fire suppression activating. It's a new ship. Got to expect some gremlins."

"Get down there and find out what's going on!" said X-20. "Both of you!"

Marina was sitting at the table in her apartment, writing quickly on a sheet of paper. She was frowning with concentration, picking her words carefully to sum up the situation as concisely as possible, but also to anticipate any questions that might arise. She finished with a decisive full stop and read through what she'd written. It would have to do. She folded the paper and hid it in her gown. Now came the bit she was dreading. She stepped over to the door and knocked gently. It opened and the white-helmeted guard looked into the apartment with a smile.

"Hey, Marina!" he said, "What can I do for you? Another videofilm?"

Marina shook her head and beckoned him into the room.

"What's the problem?" said the guard, taking a cautious step onto the carpet. He'd had strict orders from Lieutenant Coral not to enter the apartment. Marina pointed up at the central light fitting and mimed clicking it on.

"Oh I see. Bulb gone, has it?" The guard flicked the light switch by the door a few times to confirm his theory. Then he walked further into the room and looked up into the lampshade.

"Might just be loose," he said. Marina nimbly stepped around him and with the straightened fingers of her right hand, jabbed hard into the side of his neck. The poor man slumped unconscious onto the floor. Marina rarely used Pacifican Aikido, and was relieved she'd remembered where to strike. She grabbed a cushion from the sofa, carefully lifted the guard's helmeted head and slipped the cushion beneath it. She stood and looked down at him with a concerned expression. Then, very gently, he began to snore. Marina smiled with relief and headed for the door.

X-20 was all alone on Orca's bridge, sitting at the helm controls having taken over from Bahari. He experimentally pressed a button on the arm of his chair.

"Automatic bosun engaged," said a serene female voice, "Would you like to maintain the present course and speed?"

"Yes. Thank you," said X-20, and then felt silly for thanking a machine. He got up and returned to the captain's chair where he felt much more at home.

"Attention," said the automatic bosun, "Multiple craft approaching. Their course will take them past Orca at a safe distance. No action is required."

X-20 checked his instruments. Dozens of small submersibles were travelling at speed from the direction of Titanica on a course that would take them straight to Marineville's coastline. Titan's armada would not be far behind.

"Heh-heh-heh!" cackled X-20, "Everything is going according to plan! The final attack will soon begin!"

K-33 and H-27, alias Bahari and Talwar, clattered down the ladders to the bottom deck and made for the engine room with their weapons drawn.

"Beach?" called Talwar. There was no answer. They stepped over the lip of the bulkhead door and edged slowly into the room. Apart from an abandoned toolbox, there was no sign of her. Bahari lowered his gun and cast an expert eye over some dials on the wall.

"No problems here as far as I can see," he said, "Definitely no fire, anyway."

"Bahari!" said Talwar urgently. She'd pulled open a cupboard door, and as Bahari turned to look, Beach's unconscious body slid sideways out onto the deck. She'd been tied up. Bahari bent down to check her pulse. She was alive.

"Leave her. We'd better check on Hai and La Plage," said Talwar, and led the way back along the corridor and up a deck onto the portside passageway towards the galley. They slowed and crept on tiptoe as they approached the door. No sound. Talwar signalled Bahari — three, two, one, go! — and they rushed into the kitchen, guns sweeping the air in front of them to cover all the blind spots. The room was empty. Bahari lowered his gun and pulled open the larder door, and there was Hai, tied up and unconscious, sleeping peacefully on a pile of potato sacks.

"Any sign of our French friend?" said Talwar.

"No, but I think we can safely assume he's in a similar predicament, somewhere," said Bahari, "Dune must have escaped."

"Unless La Plage is a double agent?" said Talwar.

"Let's check Dune's cabin before we jump to any..."

"Shh!" said Talwar, holding up a hand. They both listened. Yes! They looked at each other and nodded. Slow footsteps in the passageway outside. Talwar and Bahari raised their guns and tiptoed to the doorway, but they must have been heard, because suddenly the footsteps were running. Talwar went through the door firing at the retreating figure, and Bahari followed her, catching a glimpse of someone in chef's whites ducking as bullets ricocheted down the corridor.

"You were right!" said Bahari, "That was La Plage!"

But Talwar wasn't convinced.

"Wearing his clothes, anyway," she said, "I'll follow him down here. You double back and take the starboard passageway. We'll have him trapped."

Troy turned a corner and skidded to a halt. He was in a shorter corridor that traversed the submarine to join the port and starboard passageways that ran either side of the reactor. One corridor led off this one at right angles to go further aft.

"Come on, come on," murmured Troy, "take the bait." Then he heard running footsteps coming towards him down the portside corridor. He peered around the corner, aimed his gun and shot twice. Talwar flattened herself to the wall and returned fire. Troy drew back, but then heard another pair of stamping boots echoing down the starboard passageway. He ran to the other corner, and shot at Bahari as he approached. The agent ducked but kept running, firing his pistol. Troy retreated and made for his only escape route – the single passageway towards the stern.

Talwar came around the corner and fired at the fleeing figure as it disappeared. Bahari joined her from the other direction.

"Did you see who it was?!" he said excitedly.

"Troy Tempest! He must have got on board this morning disguised as La Plage."

"And we've got him cornered! This passageway is a dead end. It leads to the rear dorsal airlock."

The passageway turned left, then right, then left again and Troy skidded to a halt in front of a large round hatch with a locking wheel. There was nowhere left to run. He grabbed the wheel with both hands and turned it, then pulled. He stepped back as the massive hatch swung open under its own momentum, then listened for his pursuers' approach.

Talwar and Bahari turned left, then right, then left again and skidded to a halt in front of a large round hatch that was slowly swinging shut as they approached.

"Got him!" said Talwar, and they both put their shoulders to the airlock door to close it with a clang. Bahari spun the wheel to seal the airlock, and they looked at each other and laughed.

"What a stupid place to hide," said Talwar, slipping her gun back into its holster.

"He must think we wouldn't be so cold blooded," sneered Bahari.

"But we *are* cold blooded!" replied Talwar and they both laughed again.

"Do you want to do it, or shall I?" asked Bahari. Talwar smiled.

"Be my guest."

Bahari hit a button, and through the thick metal of the hatch, they could just about hear the sound of water gushing into the airlock.

"Shame. Can't hear him screaming," said Talwar. She looked genuinely disappointed. After a short wait, there was a muffled clank which meant that the outer door had opened and the airlock was exposed to the ocean depths.

"Such frail creatures, these terraineans," said Bahari, "A few minutes under water is all it takes." He looked at his watch. "That should be long enough." He hit another button and they heard the outer door clank shut. Water gurgled as it was pumped out of the airlock, then a light above the door blinked green. Talwar spun the locking wheel, and the hatch swung open. The airlock was empty.

"The perfect end for an aquanaut. Lost at sea!" said Talwar, "Let's get back up to the bridge." And she took the lead, walking away from the airlock door and back into the narrow corridor, with Bahari following behind.

Talwar emerged from the T-junction onto the transverse passageway.

"X-20 will be annoyed," she said, "He's obsessed with Troy Tempest. He'd have wanted to see that." She looked back over her shoulder to see Bahari's reaction, but he wasn't there.

"Bahari? Agent K-33? Come on. Stop messing about." She walked back the way she'd just come: left, then right, then... at the other end of the corridor, in front of the airlock door, Troy was standing over Bahari's unconscious body and pointing his gun straight at her. At this range he couldn't miss.

"Three down, two to go," said Troy with a smile.

"But how...?" said Talwar. Without taking his eyes off her, Troy pointed upwards with his free hand. Talwar looked up at the lines of pipes and trunking that hung from brackets below the ceiling. There was just enough room for a man to swing himself up there and lie on top of them. A perfect hiding place.

"You won't take me alive!" snarled Talwar and reached for her holster. Troy instinctively pulled the trigger of his pistol, but there was an ominous click. Talwar raised her own gun and began to laugh.

"You thought you were so clever, didn't you? But now I get to kill you twice!" She pointed her pistol straight at Troy, and squeezed the trigger.

BONNNG!

Talwar collapsed in a heap, to reveal Captain Dirk Dune standing behind her with the frying pan.

"Why did you wait so long?!" shouted Troy.

"Had to pick the right dramatic moment," said Dune with a smile, "It'll make a better story down at the Blue Lagoon tonight: 'How I Saved the Day with a Cooking Utensil!'"

"But only after I'd released you from your own cabin," Troy reminded him.

"Oh, I'll miss that bit out," smirked Dune, and Troy couldn't help smiling.

"Four down, one to go," he said. "Let's get up to the bridge."

Marina was rushing through the streets of Marineville, trying to be as inconspicuous as possible. She had spent a frustrating hour trying to find Phones, but he wasn't in his apartment, he wasn't in Pen 3 with Stingray and he wasn't in the Quartermaster's store trying to find parts. Her luck was going to run out soon. So far, she'd managed to hide from any passing security guards, but the poor man she'd left snoozing in her apartment could wake up at any moment and raise the alarm. Where could Phones be? She just hoped he wasn't in the Tower, because she'd never get in there without… she stopped. But of course! There was an obvious place to look. Why hadn't she thought of it sooner? She turned around and hurried back the way she'd come.

"I mean what else would I do? Tell me, Luigi, what else would I do? Hydrophone operator. It's not exactly a transferable skill. In fact, it's more of a talent than a skill," said Phones. He was in the Blue Lagoon, slumped on a stool and leaning heavily on the bar. Luigi was standing behind it, patiently polishing glasses.

"Is that right, Lieutenant?" he said.

"Yeee-ahhh," drawled Phones, "I mean it's not just 'beep – watch out!'"

"No?"

"No!" said Phones emphatically, "You've got to listen to the tone, the volume, the freak, freak...," he frowned, "*frequency* of the beeps."

"Yes?"

"Darn right!" said Phones, "It all creates pictures in my mind's eye: 'beep' – that's a rock, 'beep, beep' – that's a bigger rock, 'beep, beep... beep'...". He tailed off, his head nodded and his eyes closed. Marina wafted quietly into the bar and hopped daintily onto the stool beside her friend. She pointed at the coffee machine and Luigi nodded.

"The Lieutenant has been here a while, Miss Marina," he said. "Apparently there's nothing wrong with Stingray that he can see, but the Commander is refusing to declare her seaworthy. He thinks he's out of a job."

Luigi placed a large black coffee in front of Marina, and she slid it along the bar to Phones until the steam was tickling his nose. His eyes opened slowly.

"Oh, hey there, Marina!" he drawled and focussed on the coffee. "Thank you. Just what I need. I've only had one drink, but it's hit me like a train. Must be tired. I was up all night, fixin' Stingray. I always seem to be fixin' Stingray."

Marina looked at Luigi who shook his head and silently held up three fingers. Marina sighed, produced the note she'd written in her apartment, and slapped it on the bar in front of Phones. He jumped.

"What's this?"

He re-focussed with difficulty and started to read. Marina watched as his eyes moved faster and faster, to and fro across the page. Then he sat bolt upright, suddenly sober.

"Jiminy!" he exclaimed.

In the Control Tower, Fisher's tracking screen suddenly lit up like a Christmas tree. He tried not to panic.

"Commander Shore!" he said, "Looks like another armoured dolphin attack! I'm reading multiple signals at extreme range – small submersible craft travelling in formation at 500 knots and heading this way!"

"How many this time?" said Shore, hovering over to join him.

"Hard to say, sir. There are so many of them, their signals are swamping our scopes. At a guess I'd say... a hundred?"

"A hundred?!" gasped Atlanta, "What can we do against a hundred of those monsters?!"

"Without Orca, we're doomed!" said Fisher.

"Battle Stations!" ordered Shore. "This could be Marineville's last stand!"

CHAPTER THIRTEEN

The Conquest of Terrainea

The invasion of the armoured dolphins was swift and terrifying. It looked like nothing could stop them this time. A hundred of the brass and steel behemoths appeared along the cliff top and swept across the open scrubland towards Marineville in a tide of destructive power. They seemed to shrug off the barrage of Interceptor missiles, sending wave after wave of rockets shooting up from the launchers on their backs to provide an impenetrable shield. Even Hydromic missiles were destroyed in mid-air, and despite the hot shrapnel that rained down over the armoured dolphins, every single one of the tried, tested and augmented mechanical beasts made it out from beneath the onslaught and thundered on, running smoothly at thirty miles per hour.

They slowed when they came to the minefield, but strode on relentlessly across the cratered landscape, raking the ground with gunfire to detonate the mines in their path. Gouts of earth shot up into the air with every explosion, and pattered down onto their helmets.

As the armoured dolphins made their final approach to Marineville's perimeter, the automated machine-gun nests activated, and bullets sparked and ricocheted off the giants' brass casings. Several of the mechanical monsters paused in their advance and took aim, each reaching out with its right arm. The fingers of the clawed hand folded back with a *snap!* to reveal the wide barrel of a grenade launcher in the wrist. The arms recoiled as they fired, and the machine-gun nests blew up, followed by a myriad of smaller explosions as the ammunition went up in flames.

And now the armoured dolphins were tearing down the fences, blue arcs of electricity sparking harmlessly around them.

"Marineville is a battlefield!" declared Commander Shore. The Tower, along with the rest of the town's central buildings, was sealed in the underground bunker, but a network of security cameras on the surface was sending disturbing images to various screens in the Control Room. All over the base, armed W.A.S.P. personnel were being driven back towards the bunker doors by the towering mechanical beasts.

"What happens if they find a way in?" said Atlanta, "We've got families down here!"

"We're about to find out!" cried Fisher, "The south door has been breached!"

Shore picked up his microphone.

"Attention! This is Marineville Control! Enemy forces have entered the bunker. I repeat, enemy forces have entered the bunker. All civilian personnel are to make their way as quickly as possible to the shelters! Go now!"

The enormous cavern of the underground bunker echoed with the crackle of gunfire. Shining mechanical giants marched through the subterranean streets, firing indiscriminately, and Marineville staff ran from them, screaming in terror.

"Marina's locked in her apartment!" said Atlanta suddenly, "She won't be able to escape!"

"The guard will get her safety," Shore reassured her, although now he came to think of it – when did he last check in?

"We could do with Marina in here," said Fisher, "she seemed to have an idea that might help us fight these creatures."

"Yes, right before Captain Dune had her arrested!" said Atlanta, "She was pointing at the PA speakers and holding her ears as though she was in pain." Atlanta looked at the various buttons and switches in front of her, searching for inspiration.

"Did she want me to broadcast some sort of message to the dolphins?" she mused.

"A message to the dolphins?!" scoffed Shore.

"Well, maybe not a message. Marina seemed to be saying it was something that would cause them pain."

Fisher clicked his fingers.

"Got it!" he exclaimed, "An ultrasonic signal! Trawlermen use ultrasound devices to keep dolphins away from their nets. The sound interferes with their hearing. It confuses them!"

Shore looked from Fisher to Atlanta.

"Do it!" he said, but Atlanta was already twisting dials, adjusting fader switches, and pressing buttons.

"Here goes nothing!" she said and then... nothing happened.

"Why isn't it working?" said Shore.

"It is!" said Atlanta, "We can't hear it, but the dolphins will! An ultrasonic signal is broadcasting from every single loudspeaker in Marineville – above and below ground!"

Outside, the firing suddenly stopped, the last shots echoing away off the walls of the bunker. Instead, a strange chittering noise filled the air, coming from the armoured dolphins. They were staggering about, holding the sides of their helmets, trying to block out the agonising ultrasonic sound. One by one, they turned and ran, more and more of them, thumping drunkenly up the stairwells and slopes to the surface, to escape the terrible noise, to escape Marineville.

"Look at 'em go!" said Shore, staring at his monitors, "They're running away! All of them!"

"Marina was right!" cried Atlanta happily.

The armoured dolphins pounded back towards the sea. Back towards freedom. They were free from that excruciating, disorientating noise. But that wasn't all. They were free from the voice in their heads that told them to do terrible things. Free from the tortuous pain that forced them to obey. And soon they would be free of these obscene suits of armour that turned them into lumbering land mammals. Soon.

They reached the cliff top, but kept running, launching themselves head first over the edge, diving in elegant arcs to splash into the cool salt water of the Pacific. They were home. But now they had work to do.

"Stand down Battle Stations, Atlanta," said Commander Shore.

"Yes, sir," replied his daughter happily, "and I have a priority call from Arago Airbase for you."

"Thanks Atlanta, put it on the speakers," said Shore.

"Marineville Control Tower from Lieutenant Coral."

"This is Commander Shore, go ahead Coral."

"Hello, sir. Are you all right? We've been following events from over here at Arago Point."

"We're all fine, Coral. We're licking our wounds, but the emergency is over."

"That's why I'm calling, sir. The emergency *isn't* over. I've been de-briefing Orca's crew. The real crew. They overheard their doppelgangers talking. The armoured dolphins were just the shock troops. The plan was for Orca to rendezvous with a fleet of Titan's Terror Fish for a follow-up attack! They were calling it, 'The Conquest of Terrainea'!"

"Atlanta! Belay my last order!" barked Shore, "Remain at Battle Stations! It seems the fight has only just begun!"

Titan's armada slowed as it approached the rendezvous coordinates. There were dozens of mechanical fish in the fleet – every vessel that Titanica had at its disposal was here, and bolstered by a bizarre assortment of craft in a wide variety of shapes, sizes and colours contributed by the other undersea races in Titan's alliance.

The largest of the submarines was another mechanical fish, but of a different

design: longer, sleeker, shaped more like a shark. This was Titan's flagship, and the Magnificent Despot himself had made the rare decision to leave Titanica, to be present at the final defeat of the despicable W.A.S.P.s.

The submarine's bridge was dominated by Titan's throne which was flanked by stone carvings of leaping fish. Why skimp on beauty, even if one was on a warship? In front of him, there were four burbling Aquaphibians who were in charge of operating the vessel. They stood in pairs at control consoles on either side of the bridge, looking out of the two large concave windows that formed the eyes of the submarine's shark design. Between the windows, there was a wide videophone screen which suddenly lit up – a call was coming through from one of the other mechanical fish.

"What is it, Sculpin?" intoned Titan, "Do you bring me news of the armoured dolphins' victory at Marineville?"

"Not exactly, your Magnificence, no," said Sculpin's green-gold face on the screen. He held up his control device for Titan to see, and gave it a little shake.

"The dolphins had breached Marineville's defences successfully, but then there was some sort of interference. I don't know what happened. I... er... I've lost contact with them." Sculpin cringed and waited for the tirade of fury.

"No matter," said Titan evenly, "The armoured dolphins achieved their main objective. Marineville will be in disarray; weak and vulnerable after the battle. And if they have defeated the dolphin shock troops, even better. They will be celebrating their victory, and will drop their guard. They will not be expecting our armada to strike and the accursed W.A.S.P.s will fall easily before our combined might!"

"If you say so," said Sculpin, and gave his control device another little shake.

"Even now," continued Titan, "Agent X-20 is bringing me the ultimate weapon! A new submarine stolen from beneath the noses of the gullible terraineans. They are deprived of its protection, and we will enjoy turning its power against them!"

"Agent H-27! Agent K-33! Report! What's going on down there?" said X-20, still waiting impatiently on Orca's bridge. They couldn't all have disappeared, he told himself. Must be a fault in the ship's Comm's systems: false fire alarm, intercom not working...

"Attention," said the calm female voice of the automatic bosun, "Multiple craft approaching. Their course and heading will intersect with that of Orca's. Please advise."

"Turn off camouflage. Maintain course, but slow to Rate One," instructed X-20.

"Camouflage System disengaged. Maintaining course. Slowing to Rate One. Ten minutes to intercept."

"Heh-heh-heh," cackled X-20, "I will lay Titan's prize at his feet, and at last I will stand at his right hand!"

"Please repeat the instruction," said the bosun.

Troy crept silently up the ladder towards the bridge until he was just below the deck. Then, very carefully, he raised his head and peered over the edge. X-20 was facing the front windows, with his back to Troy, and chuckling to himself.

"Is he there?" hissed Dune from the bottom of the ladder. Troy ducked down and waved frantically at him to be quiet. Dune apologetically put a hand over his mouth and nodded. Troy pointed at himself and then to the starboard side of the bridge; pointed at Dune and then to port.

"Pincer movement. Got you," whispered Dune. Troy flapped furiously at him to shut up. Dune mimed a zipping motion across his lips and gave a thumbs-up. Troy peeped over the edge of the deck again. X-20 still had his back to him, and was standing in front of the captain's chair, between the two steering columns, staring ahead out of the forward windows. Troy checked that his pistol was now loaded, then climbed to the top of the ladder and onto the deck. Silently, he stepped across to the starboard side. Dune also checked his pistol, and followed Troy up onto the bridge and tip-toed to port. Troy signalled Dune to stay where he was. X-20 was still oblivious to their presence, and Troy wanted to take him alive if possible. He began to creep forwards.

"Hands up, Fish-Face!" shouted Dune. X-20 spun around, saw Troy and dived behind the Weapons station. Troy fired, but the shot missed and hit the console. X-20 came up, pistol in hand, and Troy was completely exposed. They both fired at once. Another hole appeared in the Weapons console, and Troy staggered backwards.

"Aagh! He got me!" he screamed as he fell. His head hit the deck and his pistol clattered away out of reach. Dune fired several shots towards X-20's position to keep him down, and moved across to Troy. He was unconscious, but still alive.

"Attention," said a calm female voice, "Multiple ships approaching on intercept course. Action required."

"Hear that?!" shouted X-20 from his hiding place, "That's Titan and a huge armada of warships heading this way. In a few minutes we'll be surrounded. Surrender now, or die!"

Dune knelt beside Troy's inert body. There was no escape. Or was there?

"I'd never surrender to a two-faced sneak like you!" he said, and aimed a few more shots in X-20's direction. The Weapons console began to spark and fizz. While X-20 kept under cover, Dune moved as fast: he rolled Troy onto his front, grabbed him under the arms to heave him upright, and then, as Troy's unconscious body drooped forwards, Dune got a shoulder underneath him. He straightened up with Troy now carried in a fireman's lift. The training had paid off.

"Stay down, Titanican!" he shouted as fiercely as he could, and fired off a few extra shots. He carried Troy quickly to the companionway, and descended the ladder with him draped across his shoulders. X-20 risked a look over the console, and fired his gun, but they'd gone.

"Run all you like!" he shouted, "Soon Titan will be here with an army of Aquaphibians! They'll search Orca from top to bottom, root you out and then you'll pay! All terraineans will pay!" and he cackled with satisfaction until his laughter was overtaken by coughs and splutters. Smoke was rising from the Weapons console.

Orca slowed to a stop and waited as the serried ranks of Titan's huge armada emerged from the underwater gloom to face her.

Suddenly, towards the stern of Orca's hull, there was a gush of bubbles as one of the Aquapods disengaged from its socket on the port side. The upper half of the tiny submersible was an elongated glass dome, shaped like half a tear-drop, and Captain Dune peered out from the front seat, with Troy slumped in the seat behind him. The craft rose completely clear of the hull, made a sluggish one-eighty degree turn and then, very, very slowly, it began to gain speed away from Orca and the advancing line of mechanical fish.

On the bridge, X-20 was ineffectually flapping smoke away from the Weapons console and trying to blow out the smouldering controls, which was only making things worse.

"Attention," said the bosun, "Aquapod Number 2 has left Orca."

X-20 scowled.

"No! They must not escape! Green one-eighty! Turn this boat around! Now!"

"Green one-eighty," confirmed the bosun, and with a whine of hydrojets and a dizzying motion, Orca spun around on the spot. Through the front windows, X-20 watched as the view of Titan's fearsome armada slipped away to the left. Then a second later the tiny shiny dot of the Aquapod's glass dome floated in from the right.

"Target that craft!" ordered X-20, "Killer missile! Blow it out of the water!"

"Weapons System activated, Killer missile armed," said the bosun serenely.

"Heh-heh-heh!" cackled X-20, "Die Captain Dune! Die Captain Tempest! I will be rid of you at last!"

"Target acquired," reported the bosun.

"Fire!"

CHAPTER FOURTEEN

Weapons of War

A Killer missile screamed away from one Orca's four bow tubes, heading straight towards the tiny Aquapod.

A Sting missile streaked past the Aquapod in the opposite direction and met the Killer head on. A bright explosion flowered briefly in the water, and Stingray swooped through the dispersing cloud of debris, aiming straight for Orca.

On Stingray's bridge, Phones was in the captain's chair, and Marina was beside him in the co-pilot's seat, wearing his hydrophones.
"Fire missile two!" ordered Phones.

Another Sting missile darted away through the depths, and Stingray was already banking away as it hit Orca amidships and exploded.

Orca's bridge shuddered with the impact.
"What was that?!" shouted X-20.
"We are under attack," said the bosun placidly, "Damage is superficial. Would you like to initiate evasive manoeuvres and/or counter attack procedures?"

"Yes! Both! Kill them! Kill them all! Whoever they are!" said X-20 in complete panic.

"Evasive manoeuvres initiated. Weapons System calibrating. Killer missiles armed, ray guns charged, sonic cannon primed. Targets acquired."

"Fire!" screeched X-20.

Orca turned gracefully to face the nearest target and a Killer missile tore a path through the water to meet an oncoming mechanical fish right between the eyes. The fish blew apart, sending metal scales and flailing Aquaphibians spinning away in all directions.

"No!" screamed X-20, "Stop, stop, stop!"

"Cannot comply," replied the bosun evenly, "Weapons System malfunction."

X-20 launched himself at the smoking Weapons console and stabbed the melted buttons with increasing desperation, but nothing was happening. The controls were too badly damaged.

Orca spun crazily in a circle, Killer missiles shooting like fireworks out of all four bow tubes. Thin red beams of deadly light fanned out in every direction, and the sonic cannon kept throbbing deep pulses of infrasound in a slow, steady beat, sending out ripples in cones of expanding circles. Titan's armada was being decimated, as vessels were blown up by the missiles, sliced into little pieces by the ray guns or shaken apart by the sonic cannon. The fleet scattered in every direction to escape the chaos.

In all the confusion, Stingray had caught up with the Aquapod and had reduced speed to cruise alongside it, slowly but surely gaining more and more distance from the mayhem behind them.

"Even if we jettison one of our Aquasprites," Phones was talking on the radio, "the Aquapod's too big to fit into the socket. You'll have to try and make a seal over our forward airlock. But make it quick!"

"P.W.O.R!" said Dune's voice.

On Orca's bridge, X-20 was kneeling in front of the Weapons console, pulling out circuit boards from beneath the control panel, and tugging wires from their connections in big clumps. Alarms were going off and the deck pitched and swayed as Orca manoeuvred to acquire yet another target.

"I have completely lost control of the situation," said the bosun soothingly. X-20 grabbed hold of a thick red cable and yanked one end free from the console. There was a bright white flash.

"Weapons System offline," reported the bosun, "All stop," and Orca finally came to rest.

"Are we still under attack?" said X-20.

"Negative. Hydrophone readings indicate a single attacker on a retreating course, engine signature consistent with W.A.S.P. submarine Stingray."

"Stingray!" X-20 spat the hated word, "Why does Stingray always ruin my plans?"

"Insufficient information," said the bosun. The videophone screen in front of the captain's chair flickered on.

"Agent X-20! You imbecile! You cretin! You moron!"

It was Titan, calling from his flagship which, it seemed, had survived. X-20 scrambled up into his chair to reply.

"Oh Merciful Titan!" he said, "I have delivered Orca into your hands!"

"You have destroyed or damaged nearly half my fleet!"

"Oh Beneficent Titan! It was the despicable Troy Tempest, and the contemptible Dirk Dune! They somehow managed to incapacitate my crew and sabotage Orca. But I bravely fought them off and they fled in an escape pod."

"Then we must pursue and kill them!"

"But Impetuous Titan! Stingray is here!"

"Oh," said Titan. He thought for a moment. "Then I will make a strategic withdrawal. The remains of my fleet will do the pursuing and killing."

The screen went blank.

Troy was coming round as Dune and Marina helped him down through Stingray's forward hatch and into the airlock where they leant him up against the wall.

"Oh, hey Marina!" he said, groggily, then his eyes widened. "Say, this is Stingray!" He slid down the wall and sat heavily on the floor. "Someone shot me. Just a scratch. Fell over. Hit my head." He rambled on while Marina examined the wound in his side. There was a lot of blood, but it looked like the bullet had gone straight through. Dune climbed back up through the hatch into the Aquapod, which was sitting neatly on top of Stingray's prow like a huge limpet. He hit a button and quickly descended again into the airlock, sealing the hatch above him.

"That's it, I've activated the automatic release, and the Aquapod will jettison in… well, any second now."

And they all ducked as a loud thud of equalising pressure told them that the Aquapod had released its hold.

"Let's get up to the bridge," said Dune, "Time we got out of here."

Sculpin was on one of the surviving mechanical fish, still trying to figure out what had gone wrong with his control device, while the Aquaphibian pilots attempted to re-group with what remained of the fleet. Sculpin couldn't understand it. The device should still work. The circular aerial on top was still rotating. It was still transmitting. Surely the armoured suits couldn't all have failed at the same time? It didn't make sense.

The deck pitched slightly as the Terror Fish came about onto a new heading.

"What's happening?" he said.

"We have orders to pursue and destroy Stingray!" burbled one of the Aquaphibians.

"Come on, come on, time's a-wastin'," said Phones as Marina and Dune helped a very pale Troy onto the sofa at the rear of Stingray's bridge. Dune came forward and went to sit beside Phones in the hydrophone operator's chair, but Phones shook his head.

"Oh no you don't, Captain. That seat is taken."

And Marina gently pushed Dune aside and sat down. She buckled in, placed the hydrophone headset over her ears and gave Phones a thumbs-up.

"Well then... I'd better see to Captain Tempest's wound," said Dune with magnificent dignity, and retreated to the lounge area.

Stingray accelerated away from the drifting Aquapod, but behind them, a dozen mechanical fish were already in pursuit, and more of the remaining fleet were altering course to join the chase.

Marina urgently tapped her steering wheel.

"What have we got, Marina?" said Phones, and she held up five fingers and waggled her hand. Their symbol for...

"Too many to tell, eh?" said Phones and Marina nodded, then pointed aft.

"And right on our tail. Cross your fingers," said Phones, and Marina did, holding them up for him to see. He grinned.

"Acceleration Rate Six!" he announced and pushed the throttle lever all the way forward. There was a loud bang, and a thick cloud of choking black smoke rose from a blown-out panel.

"That's impossible!" wailed Phones, "I went over every inch of those engines myself!"

The note of the turbine wound down as Stingray slowed to a halt, and began to drift.

"It's not the engine!" shouted Dune, who was busy with a fire extinguisher at the smoking panel, "The problem's up here."

"What do you mean?" yelled Phones. Dune put down the fire extinguisher and moved quickly to an inspection panel right at the front of the cabin.

"I have a confession to make," he said, as he removed the panel, "On a previous visit to Stingray, I did a spot of rewiring to bypass the throttle regulator..."

"...So it would blow all the fuses every time we pushed the engines too quickly," completed Phones, who was already out of his seat and opening his toolkit. "And there was I, thinking the engines were overloading the circuits. It was just the throttle."

"Why would you do that?" said Troy. He had come up behind them, pulling a uniform jacket on over his bandaged torso. He was still pale, but looking more like his usual self. Dune shrugged.

"I thought that with Stingray out of action, and not using up valuable resources, Project Orca was more likely to succeed," he explained.

"Get out of my way," said Phones, and he shouldered Dune aside to get at the exposed components.

"Troy! We haven't got time to change all the fuses," he said as he worked, "so we'll have to risk it and take a leaf out of Captain Dune's book...."

"...And bypass them. P.W.O.R!" said Troy, and he tackled the blackened panel with a screwdriver.

Marina tapped her steering wheel again, and they all turned to look at her. She was pointing out of the starboard window. Stingray had drifted round, and now they had a perfect view of an advancing line of Terror Fish, closing in for the kill.

"We're too late!" cried Troy.

But suddenly, from all directions, armoured dolphins appeared, streaking like torpedoes through the water, converging on the enemy vessels and firing at them.

"Wondered where they'd got to," said Phones, "Must have been circling the fleet. Getting into position. Surrounding them."

"Why are they attacking their own vessels? Have they changed sides?" wondered Dune.

"Beats me, but they're buying us some time – keep working!" ordered Troy. Marina walked to the window and watched the dolphins weave in and out between the scattering mechanical fish, firing at will. She clapped her hands happily. The dolphins were finally free, and they were exacting their revenge.

The dolphins wanted nothing more than to rid themselves of the profane armoured suits, but it seemed fitting that they should be used one last time, against the people who had captured, imprisoned and operated on dolphin-kind, linking them via surgical implants to weapons of war, forcing them against their will to commit terrible acts of destruction.

The suits were still receiving signals from the one who inflicted unbearable pain upon them, and it was a simple matter to track the signal to its source. They had encircled the fleet of metal abominations, the cruel parodies of marine life that polluted the oceans with their stink, and had commenced their attack. Now they were searching for the one vessel that contained the cause of all their suffering.

Sculpin's Terror Fish powered towards Stingray, the Aquaphibian pilots burbling excitedly to each other. The round windows lit up with the flash of an explosion, and the deck shuddered beneath their feet.

"We're under attack!" Sculpin shrieked, "Get us out of here!"

But the pilots didn't seem to hear him; they were consumed by the thrill of the chase.

"Stingray is adrift!" gurgled one of the Aquaphibians, "It will soon be in range! Prepare to fire missiles!"

Suddenly, Sculpin's control device emitted a loud insistent beeping. He snatched it up and looked at the readings. At last! Thank Teufel! It was working! The armoured dolphins had returned!

On Orca's bridge, X-20 was considering his options when the armoured dolphins attacked the remains of Titan's fleet. His crew seemed to have disappeared, he had no weapons, and he wasn't even sure he had a job anymore.

"Turn on the camouflage!" he ordered, hoping that it was on a different circuit to the Weapons System.

"Camouflage System engaged," said the automatic bosun. X-20 breathed a deep sigh of relief. Orca was now invisible to both friend and foe.

"Get me out of here," he said.

"Please state course heading and speed."

"As far away from here as possible, and as quick as you can!"

"Evasive course locked in, Rate Six point Five," confirmed the bosun, and Orca was already turning to a new heading, and powering away from the battle.

"I'll give Titan a day or so to calm down," said X-20 to himself. "He'll have reflected on the situation and realised that the damage to his fleet is all the fault of Troy Tempest. And that toadying fool Sculpin with his technological tampering. And not forgetting my incompetent crew, wherever they are – dead or tied up down below, I suppose. They can stay there, for all I care. I'll return single-handed to Titanica if I have to, present King Titan with Orca and be given a hero's welcome! But not quite yet."

Troy dropped his tools onto Stingray's deck and dusted off his hands.

"I've finished here," he said, "How's it looking at your end, Phones?"

"Nearly there," he replied, "Get ready to go!"

Troy dropped into his usual seat with a wince of pain, and Marina took her place beside him.

"How did you find me, Phones?" said Troy, as his friend continued his frantic rewiring.

"Marina was the only person you told about your crazy plan to stowaway on Orca," said Phones without looking up, "so when she heard that Orca had disappeared, she assumed the worst and came to tell me. Didn't have a clue how to locate you, so we followed the armoured dolphins when they left Marineville, figuring they'd be on their way to wherever the action was. Didn't expect them to have changed sides though."

Marina shook her head. She knew that the dolphins had never really been against them.

"Er... fellas?" said Dune. One of the Terror Fish had escaped the battle with the armoured dolphins and was almost upon them. As they watched, its huge mouth dropped open to reveal a missile tube.

The dolphins had located the source of their pain. They formed a wide circle around one of the mechanical fish then dived towards it.

"Finished!" said Phones, "Hit it!"
"Acceleration Rate Six!" said Troy and pushed the throttle lever all the way forward.

The whine of Stingray's turbine rose in pitch and she turned her stern towards the approaching Terror Fish, and accelerated away, just as a missile launched from the Fish's gaping mouth.

Armoured dolphins appeared from every direction, firing upon the Terror Fish with everything they had, until...

KA-BOOM!

...it tore apart in a huge and colourful explosion.
The dolphins gracefully peeled off and powered away from the scattered vessels of Titan's fleet. They had exacted their revenge and now, at last, they could shed their armour. The glass helmets hinged back, the long brass torsos split open, and the dolphins' sinuous bodies wriggled out, wires and tubes detaching from the surgically implanted sockets that they would bear for life. But they could feel the water on their skins once more, and they were free. Twisting and weaving around each other in exultation, they swam away, leaving the armoured suits to sink slowly to the ocean bed, to join the wreckage of the mechanical fish that had held Sculpin and his control device.

Stingray still had a missile on her tail. She headed straight for a rocky outcrop, and with the missile almost upon her, suddenly corkscrewed away to port. The missile hit the rocks and exploded.

"Marineville here we come!" said Troy.

"What are we going to do about Captain Sabotage back there?" said Phones, who was standing beside Marina's chair. Captain Dune was sitting on the sofa behind them.

"Well, he did save my life," said Troy, "I wouldn't have escaped Orca without him."

Dune stepped forward to stand beside Troy.

"Just returning the favour," he said quietly. "If you hadn't stowed away on board Orca, I'd be in Titan's hands or dead by now. It was a very brave thing to do. When did you realise that my crew were all enemy agents?"

Troy didn't answer for a moment. Then he seemed to come to a decision.

"You owned up to sabotaging Stingray," he said, "so I suppose I should own up too." He looked across at Marina who smiled and nodded.

"I had no idea they were all enemy agents. I was angry and wanted to get back at you. My plan was to sabotage Orca so you'd have to be towed back to Marineville, like Stingray was. I wanted you to know how it felt. To be humiliated. I went to Henri La Plage and I was going to ask to take his place, explain it away as a Marineville joke, a sort of initiation ceremony or something, but as soon as I got through the door, he pulled a gun on me! I had to knock him out and put him in the bath. Then I realised I was already wearing my false moustache, and he must have thought I was a spy and panicked. I just thought he was being a loyal W.A.S.P officer. I didn't know he was a Titanican Surface Agent! By then I figured I was in enough trouble already and decided to go through with my plan."

"Well of all the lowdown..." began Dune, and then began to laugh. Troy and Phones joined in with relief.

"The person we should all be thanking is Marina," said Troy, "We'd both be sunk if it weren't for her."

"Thank you, Marina," said Dune, "I have to admit, I was wrong about you." Everyone turned to look at him in surprise.

"Gee, Captain Dune," said Phones, "It's mighty big of you to admit that."

"But tell anyone I said so, and I shall deny it," finished Dune.

EPILOGUE
Undersea Friends

Commander Shore had called a meeting. Once again, he took his place at the head of the Plotting Room table in Marineville's Control Tower. He looked around at the brave men and women of the World Aquanaut Security Patrol he was proud to have served with during the recent crisis – people he knew he could rely on in the continuing fight against the forces of Titanica: Captain Troy Tempest, Marina of Pacifica, and Lieutenants Phones Sheridan, John Fisher, Sara Coral and of course, his precious daughter, Atlanta Shore.

Captain Dirk Dune had been recalled to Washington by Admiral Stern – good riddance to him – and the rest of Orca's crew had returned to their posts around the world, but not before Henri La Plage, the real Henri La Plage, had cooked them all a fabulous dinner. Now it was back to work.

"I think we are in agreement that the situation is dire," said Commander Shore. "Orca has disappeared and we must assume that the world's most advanced submarine is in enemy hands. But thanks to the brave intervention of Captain Tempest..." Phones coughed pointedly, and Troy blushed "...we know there was a weapons malfunction on board, and that many of Titan's fleet were destroyed in the ensuing confusion. And thanks to Marina..."

Atlanta gave her a little round of applause.

"...the armoured dolphins were repelled, and as far as we can make out, they then turned on their masters. In the light of how things turned out, I have decided to overlook Marina's attack on a security guard. He is too embarrassed to press charges anyway."

It was Marina's turn to blush.

"In my report to W.S.P. Headquarters, I have also failed to mention the unauthorised launch of Stingray by Marina and Lieutenant Sheridan."

"Gee, thanks, Commander," said Phones, "But if we hadn't launched and followed the armoured dolphins, Troy wouldn't be sitting here right now."

"Don't push your luck, Phones," growled Shore. But he was smiling.

"We survived the battle," the Commander continued, "but Titan will re-group, and his deadly uprising will continue. We must be ready."

A glum silence fell over the room. Then Troy straightened in his seat and looked at Marina. She gave him a resolute nod. Then he looked at Phones. He also nodded. Troy took a deep breath.

"If I may, sir?" he began, and Shore waved at him to continue.

"I think recent events have made it clear that Marineville is vulnerable. The World Aquanaut Security Patrol was almost defeated. The alliances that Titan has made with the other undersea races have brought him unlimited resources that enable him to keep attacking us. We can't hold out against him forever. We can't do this on our own. But why should we? There are many undersea races that hate Titan and what he's doing, so it's time to ask for their help. To make alliances of our own."

There was another brief silence while Shore considered Troy's words, and then he spoke.

"It's a good notion, Tempest, but the undersea races are afraid of reprisals. Titan has them in his grip and they're likely to act unpredictably."

"Nevertheless, sir – and with respect – I think we should try. I've talked it over with Phones and Marina, and we're volunteering to take Stingray on a mission to enlist the help of our undersea friends, and bring the fight to Titan."

"Very well," said Commander Shore. "Project Orca may have been a failure, but I know that I can always put my trust in Stingray and her crew. Good luck."

Nothing. Again. X-20 wearily turned his little red and green submarine onto the next heading and continued the search. He watched the scopes carefully while muttering to himself in a bad impression of the Vainglorious Titan's pompous voice.

"There's a bit missing, X-20. Go and search for it, X-20. Don't come back until you've found it, X-20."

X-20's return to Titanica had not matched his dreams of a hero's welcome. As soon as Orca had docked, his disgruntled crew had got off the submarine as quickly as they could – mainly to get away from X-20 – only to be met by a squad of Aquaphibians who had led them away in shame. Quite right too, X-20 had thought, for allowing the contemptible Tempest to get the better of them. Their failure had nothing to do with him.

But when he'd disembarked by himself a little later, he'd been met in the airlock by two more Aquaphibians who had escorted him straight to the throne room under guard. Titan had ranted at him for a good ten marine minutes. He'd blamed the accursed Tempest for causing Orca's weapons system to go haywire; he'd blamed the incompetent Sculpin for losing control of the armoured dolphins; but most of all he'd blamed X-20 because X-20 was there to face Titan's wrath, while Tempest and Sculpin weren't. It wasn't fair.

And then, when Titan had finally taken a travel tube to gaze upon Orca, the latest and most impressive addition to his arsenal, he'd blamed X-20 some more. Titan had the world's most advanced submarine at his disposal, and all he could do was complain that one of the escape pods was missing.

And so it was that X-20 had returned to the battlefield and the area where Aquaphibian survivors had last reported seeing the Aquapod adrift. So far, he'd spent two very long days scouring the ocean depths without result. He checked the scope. Nothing. Again. X-20 sighed, turned his submarine onto the next heading and continued the search.

The End

OTHER GREAT TITLES
BY ANDERSON ENTERTAINMENT

available from
shop.gerryanderson.com

STINGRAY

Stingray: Operation Icecap
by John Theydon

The Stingray crew discover an ancient diving bell that leads them on an expeditionary voyage through the freezing waters of Antarctica to the land of a lost civilisation.

Close on the heels of Troy Tempest and the pride of the World Aquanaut Security Patrol is the evil undersea ruler Titan. Ahead of them are strange creatures who inhabit underground waterways and an otherworldly force with hidden powers strong enough to overwhelm even Stingray's defences.

Stingray: Monster from the Deep
by John Theydon

Commander Shore's old enemy, Conrad Hagen, is out of prison and back on the loose with his beautiful but devious daughter, Helga. When they hijack a World Aquanaut Security Patrol vessel and kidnap Atlanta, it's up to Captain Troy Tempest and the crew of Stingray to save her.

But first they will have to uncover the mystery of the treasure of Sanito Cathedral and escape the fury of the monster from the deep.

Stingray: The Titanican Stratagem
By Chris Dale

A daring raid on Marineville is merely the first stage in an audacious scheme by Titan to achieve final victory over the terraineans! The undersea despot is hunting for new allies – but has he made a fatal mistake with the first recruits to his cause?

As the Stingray crew deals with the fallout of Titan's latest scheme, the team at Marineville – including new arrival Lieutenant Sara Coral – embarks on a rescue mission to save them, but some old enemies are about to intervene in the war between Marineville and Titanica – and the result could be the obliteration of all sides!

Five Star Five: John Lovell and the Zargon Threat
by Richard James

THE TIME: THE FUTURE
THE PLACE: THE UNIVERSE

The peaceful planet of Kestra is under threat. The evil Zargon forces are preparing to launch a devastating attack from an asteroid fortress. With the whole Kestran system in the Zargons' sights, Colonel Zana looks to one man to save them. Except one man isn't enough.

Gathering a crack team around him including a talking chimpanzee, a marauding robot and a mystic monk, John Lovell must infiltrate the enemy base and save Kestra from the Zargons!

Five Star Five: The Doomsday Device
by Richard James

THE TIME: THE FUTURE
THE PLACE: THE UNIVERSE

The Zargon home world is dying. With their nemesis in prison on trumped up charges, they have developed a brand-new weapon of awesome power.

As the Zargons plot another attempt on the planet Kestra, a group of friends must band together and rescue their only hope for survival – John Lovell!

Five Star Five: The Battle for Kestra
by Richard James

THE TIME: THE FUTURE
THE PLACE: THE UNIVERSE

As the Zargons prepare their last, desperate attempt to invade their enemy planet, John Lovell and his gang of misfits stand accused of acts of terror on Kestran soil.

With a new President in place, the 'Five Star Five' are forced underground before they can confront the enemy within and thwart the Zargons' plans.

A GERRY ANDERSON PRODUCTION

THUNDERBIRDS

Thunderbirds: Terror from the Stars
by John Theydon

Thunderbird Five is attacked by an unknown enemy with uncanny powers. An unidentified object is tracked landing in the Gobi desert, but what's the connection? Scott Tracy races to the scene in the incredible Thunderbird One, but he cannot begin to imagine the terrible danger he is about to encounter.

Alone in the barren wilderness, he is possessed by a malevolent intelligence and assigned a fiendish mission – one which, if successful, will have the most terrifying consequences for the entire world.

International Rescue are about to face their most astounding adventure yet!

Thunderbirds: Peril in Peru
by John Theydon

An early warning of disaster brings International Rescue to Peru to assist in relief efforts following a series of earth tremors – and sends the Thunderbirds in search of an ancient Inca treasure trove hidden beneath a long-lost temple deep in the South American jungle!

When Lady Penelope is kidnapped by sinister treasure hunters, Scott Tracy and Parker are soon hot on their trail.

Along the way they'll have to solve a centuries-old mystery, brave the inhospitable wilderness of the jungle and even tangle with a lost tribe – with the evil Hood close behind them all the way...

Thunderbirds: Operation Asteroids
by John Theydon

What starts out as a simple rescue mission to save a trapped miner on the Moon, soon turns out to be one of International Rescue's greatest catastrophes. After the Hood takes members of International Rescue hostage during the rescue, a chase across space and an altercation among the asteroids only worsens the situation.

With the Hood hijacking Thunderbird Three along with Brains, Lady Penelope and Tin-Tin, it is up to the Tracy brothers to stage a daring rescue in the mountain tops of his hidden lair.

But can they rescue Brains before his engineering genius is used for the destructive forces of evil?

SPACE: 1999

SPACE: 1999 Maybe There – The Lost Stories from SPACE: 1999
by David Hirsch & Robert E. Wood

Strap into your Moon Ship and prepare for a trip to an alternate universe!

Gathered here for the first time are the original stories written in the early days of production on the internationally acclaimed television series SPACE: 1999. Uncover the differences between Gerry and Sylvia Anderson's original story Zero G, George Bellak's first draft of The Void Ahead and Christopher Penfold's uncredited shooting script Turning Point. Each of these tales shows the evolution of the pilot episode with scenes and characters that never made it to the screen.

Wonder at a tale that was NEVER filmed where the Alpha People, desperate to migrate to a new home, instigate a conflict between two alien races. Also included are Christopher Penfold's original storylines for Guardian of Piri and Dragon's Domain, an adaption of Keith Miles's early draft for All That Glisters and read how Art Wallace (Dark Shadows) originally envisioned the episode that became Matter of Life and Death.

Discover how SPACE: 1999 might have been had they gone 'Maybe There?'

The Armageddon Engine
by James Swallow

Adrift in deep space, Commander John Koenig and the people of Moonbase Alpha face an uncertain fate when a planet-killing alien weapon at the heart of a sinister cloud diverts their lost Moon on to a fatal trajectory.

As each moment brings the Moon closer to total obliteration, Koenig leads a desperate mission into the unknown to save all life on Alpha. Does hope lie among a rag-tag colony of refugees hiding in the shadow of devastation? Or can the Alphans find a path into the heart of the war machine and end its destructive rampage? With time running out, the answer will mean the difference between survival... or annihilation.

Intergalactic Rescue 4: Stellar Patrol
by Richard James

It is the 22nd century. The League of Planets has tasked Jason Stone, Anne Warran and their two robots, Alpha and Zeta to explore the galaxy, bringing hope to those in need of rescue.

On board Intergalactic Rescue 4, they travel to ice moons and jungle planets in 10 exciting adventures that see them journey further across the stars than anyone before.

But what are the secret transmissions that Anne discovers?

And why do their rescues seem to be taking them on a predetermined course?

Soon, Anne discovers that her co-pilot, Jason, might be on a quest of his own...

FIRST ACTION BUREAU

Damaged Goods
by Richard James

First Action Bureau exists to protect the Earth from criminal elements before they get the chance to act. Using decades of 'big data' and globally connected quantum artificial intelligence, First Action Bureau is able to predict criminal activity before it occurs...

Nero Jones has led a troubled life, but things are about to get a whole lot worse... Press-ganged into joining First Action Bureau, a shadowy organisation set up to counter terrorist threats, Nero finds herself thrown into a range of increasingly more exciting missions under the guidance of the mysterious Nathan Drake.

As she learns more about the Bureau, she's haunted by half-forgotten memories that lead her to question everything she knows. Just what is real and what is fake? As she delves deeper into the Bureau's history, she comes to a startling conclusion; nothing is true!

UFO

Shadow Play
by James Swallow

The last line of defence in a clandestine war, SHADO is all that stands between humanity and a force of alien invaders – and leading that fight is the uncompromising Ed Straker, commanding Earth's defenders around the clock. But what happens when the man at the top is pushed too far?

After an experiment goes wrong, Straker awakens from a coma with missing memories and strange hallucinations that threaten his grip on reality – but is it the result of alien interference, or has the commander's iron will finally cracked?

Facing danger from within and without, Straker must find the truth... even if it kills him.